DANNY ORLIS
AND
JIM'S NORTHERN ADVENTURE

DANNY ORLIS

AND

JIM'S NORTHERN ADVENTURE

BERNARD PALMER

Please note that several books in the Danny Orlis series are published by Sword of the Lord Publications and are available for purchase on their website, www.swordbooks.com.

CONTENTS

CHAPTER 1

NORTH TO CANADA

Spring came to Minnesota with a rush. The snow melted. Fresh new leaves clothed the forests. And the kids in school looked longingly to the day when they would take their final exams and get out for the summer. Jim Morgan was no different than the others. He had been wanting to get a job for the two or three summer months but hadn't been able to find anything.

"I don't know what the trouble is, Danny," he said, discouragement creeping into his voice. "I've been everywhere and tried everything I can think of, but there doesn't seem to be any work for a fellow my age."

Danny put aside his magazine. "I wouldn't worry about it if I were you."

Jim's head snapped up. "Do you know where there's a job where I can earn a little money?"

Danny shook his head. "Not exactly."

"What do you mean by that?"

"Suppose you just take it easy for a week or so," the pilot told him, turning back to his magazine.

Jim got up and went back to the kitchen where Kay was fixing supper.

"I'd like to talk to you."

"About anything in particular?" Her eyes were dancing.

"That's what I want to find out."

She took the meat off the stove and put it on the table. "You're talking in riddles, Jim," she said.

Exasperation gleamed in his eyes.

"I want to know what's going on here," he said. "You and Danny both act as though you've got some big, dark secret."

"Do we?" She smiled again.

"Come on, Kay," he pleaded. "Tell me what's going on, won't you?"

"Is there something going on?"

"For cryin' out loud! You're as bad as Danny!" She did not answer him.

Jim tried several times during the next few days to question Danny and Kay, but it was no use. Neither of them would tell him anything.

"I think you're kidding me, Danny."

"About what?"

"You know."

"Do I? That's interesting."

In disgust Jim gave up.

A few days later Danny left for a month of flying and Jim still didn't know what he had been talking about. Two weeks after Danny had left, Jim came home from a late baseball practice to find Kay in the living room.

"I'm sorry I'm late," he said. "We had an extra-long baseball session today. I hope you didn't wait on me."

"I don't like to eat alone, Jim," she said, starting toward the kitchen. "I have everything ready. It'll only take a couple of minutes to get supper on the table."

"Hear from Danny today?"

She shook her head. "No, but you got a letter from Ron and Darlene."

"I did?" His eyes widened. "Why would they write to me?"

"The letter's in on the dining room table."

He found it and hurriedly opened it. As he read, a broad smile lifted the corners of his mouth.

"How are they?" Kay asked.

"OK, I guess." His eyes gleamed. "Do you know what Ron wants?"

She laughed pleasantly. "Does Ron want something?"

Jim scarcely heard her question. He was scanning the letter once more.

"He says that some of the fellows from Cedarton Bible Institute (CBI) are going up to his station this summer to help build a cabin for the Indian evangelist who's going to be working with him and Darlene," he said. His smile broke out once more. "And guess what? He wants me to come up and help them!"

"That sounds interesting."

"Interesting?" he exclaimed. "It'd be just about the greatest vacation a guy ever had. And besides, we'd be doing something for the Lord."

She continued to work in the kitchen without answering.

In a moment, his gaze met hers accusingly.

"You and Danny have known all about this for a long time, haven't you?" he demanded.

"What makes you think that?"

"You can't fool me anymore. I know you have."

"Well, we did hear something about it."

"I knew it."

"You see," she went on, "they wrote and asked if we thought it would be all right to invite you."

"You told them I could go, didn't you?"

A deep frown chased away her smile.

"I think maybe Danny has had plans for you for the summer."

Jim groaned inwardly. And then he saw the merriment twinkling in her eyes. "Aw, Kay. You're just kidding."

"As a matter of fact, Danny did have plans for you," she said. "But when he got Ron's letter, he thought that going north for the summer would be much better for you."

* * *

The letter from Ron and Darlene had been delayed a week or more, it turned out, and there wasn't much time for Jim to get ready. The very next morning Kay started washing his clothes and helping him get his gear lined up. Two days later he took the bus to Cedarton so he could ride north with the Bible school students who were also going up to Ron and Darlene's.

Harold Forester met him at the bus depot and took him out to the school where he met Wade Fessler, Ernie Jensen and Ray Spear. The Bible school fellows already were packed and planned to leave in Ray's old car that very night.

"We're sure glad you got here this afternoon," Wade said. "We're all set to go."

Jim looked them over carefully. They were a little older than him, and had the same clean, fresh look of most Bible school fellows; there was the same square cut to their shoulders and the same determination in their manner. He knew instinctively that it was going to be great spending the summer with them.

"It sure is going to be good to see old Ron again," he said to no one in particular.

When they had their gear in the car and were headed north, Wade and his friends began to question Jim about the place where Ron and Darlene lived.

"Has he written home about the people he and Darlene are living among?"

"A little."

"What're they like?"

"They don't say too awfully much about them; but to tell you the truth, it doesn't sound as though anyone up there is very friendly."

Ray broke in. "I've been wondering about that. When Ron wrote and asked us to come up, he said that it wouldn't be any picnic for us. It sounds as though they're left pretty much alone."

Jim nodded.

"Danny and I were talking about it a couple of times. I guess Danny has been in there a few times since they've started to work. He said there's quite a lot of opposition among the people. They don't like strangers, and as far as they're concerned Ron and Darlene are outsiders and they don't want to have anything to do with them."

"I suppose they'll be antagonistic toward us too," he said.

Jim slowly expelled his breath. That was something he hadn't considered. In spite of what Danny had said, somehow he'd always figured that everybody loved missionaries. The fact that they might run into opposition was something entirely new. Uneasiness crept over him.

They headed northwest out of Cedarton toward the Canadian border. By noon the following day they were well into Saskatchewan. At midnight they pulled into the little community that served as mission headquarters. The executive director, Bob Selko, met them and showed them their rooms.

"We're so glad you fellows were able to come and help Ron with this building project," he said. "Without your help I'm afraid he wouldn't have been able to get it finished before cold weather."

Jim grinned. "How soon are we going to get to go to High Rock? That's what I want to know."

"When we got your text that you were leaving Minnesota, we made arrangements for the aircraft to stand by. We'll fly two of you in tomorrow and the other two the next day."

Jim spoke up quickly. "Dibs on going first."

"Nothing doing," Ray protested. "You'll draw straws and take your chances with the rest of us."

The mission superintendent started to leave the room. "I think we'd all better get some sleep," he said. "The pilot plans on taking off at six in the morning."

Jim was so excited he didn't think he would be able to sleep that night. But he was more exhausted than he supposed. He lay back on the bed and closed his eyes; the next thing he knew, it was morning. Wade was grasping his shoulder and shaking him.

"Jim!" he said. "Wake up! What're you going to do? Sleep all day?"

He shook his head and scrubbed at his eyes with his fists. "What's the big idea of wakin' me up in the middle of the night?" he demanded.

"Middle of the night, nothin'! Open your eyes and look around, will you?"

It was as bright in the room as it would have been

at noon. Jim leaped hurriedly from the bed and scrambled into his clothes.

"What happened? Did we all oversleep?"

His companion laughed.

"It's five-fifteen. Time to get dressed so we can have breakfast and be on our way."

"What about drawing straws?"

"We already did, and you won, you lucky stiff."

Jim grinned broadly. "Imagine that! I won and I didn't know anything about it."

Mr. Selko took them down to the lake after breakfast and introduced them to the pilot who was to fly them to Ron's station.

Jim got into the front seat with him.

"Have you ever been where Ron and Darlene live, Mr. Dunbar?" he asked.

The pilot's grin was infectious.

"I get to all the stations. But don't call me Mr. Dunbar," he said. "The name's Harry."

"Sure thing, Harry."

"Yes, I've been to Ron's station many times. In fact, I was there even before anyone thought about opening a mission station."

There was a brief silence.

"What's it like?"

His face grew hard. "It's tough," he said. "It's mighty tough."

The boy eyed him curiously. "What do you mean by that?" he asked.

"Just exactly what I said. There's a lot of drinking and gambling and fighting – more than I've ever seen in any isolated settlement, and I get into most of them at one time or another. The people are hardened to the gospel. In fact, they're violently opposed to it."

Jim ran a hand uneasily across his face. Ron had hinted that it wasn't easy at High Rock, but he had never indicated it was as difficult as the pilot said.

"How many converts does he have?"

The pilot shook his head.

"None. Absolutely none. And from the way Ron talked the last time I was in there, nobody will even listen to him when he tries to talk with them. It's tough, all right."

CHAPTER 2

COLD RECEPTION

The missionary pilot let the engine of the trim little floatplane warm up, then he taxied out to the center of the lake.

Jim turned to him with a look of curiosity on his face. "How far is it to High Rock where Ron and Darlene are stationed?"

The pilot pulled thoughtfully at the lobe of his ear. "Let's see. It takes about three quarters of an hour to fly up there. I'd say it's between ninety and a hundred miles."

Ernie, who was sitting in the back with their luggage, leaned forward intently. "Do you mean that we'll be that far from a road?"

The pilot laughed. "You'll be that far from a road," he said. "And to tell you the truth, you'll be that far from anything else that smacks of civilization as you're used to it, except for aircraft and radio."

The Bible school student pursed his lips. "I sure didn't expect anything like that." he exclaimed.

Mr. Dunbar grinned. "Want to back out?"

"Me, back out? I should say not. I wouldn't miss this for anything."

Jim spoke up quickly. "Neither would I."

"I've been flying in this country for more than three years," the pilot said, "and I still find it as fascinating as I did on the very first trip."

There was a brief silence. Finally, Ernie spoke once more. "What's it like?"

Mr. Dunbar frowned. "It's just trees and lakes and rivers with a bunch of rocks thrown in."

"That doesn't sound very fascinating."

"That's the strange thing about it," the missionary pilot acknowledged. "And I'll tell you frankly, I don't understand why it's so fascinating. But it is. It has a way of getting into your blood that defies explanation."

"That's what Danny says. He told me that there's an old saying among people of the north. 'He who tastes of the waters of the north will return to drink again.'"

"That's about as good a way of putting it as any. I know I've fallen in love with the country."

The missionary pilot inched the plane upward to an altitude of a thousand feet. The green of the forests and the glimmering blue of the lakes and streams were interwoven in exquisite patterns. From horizon to horizon the sky was cloudless, and the wind was so slight it scarcely dimpled the water below. There was no visible evidence that anyone had ever been on the terrain they were flying over. Surely no one had ever lived there, so desolate it appeared.

Neither Ernie nor Jim spoke much. They sat in awe, staring out the cabin windows. After a time, Jim saw a moose standing knee-deep in the water. Half around the lake was a second dark object he took to be a bear. Looking back at Ernie, he pointed down; but the other boy couldn't see anything. Jim wasn't even sure a moment later that he had.

The two boys continued to study the changing scene below. Both were so intent that they were surprised when the aircraft began to lose altitude.

Jim stood erect. "What's up?"

Mr. Dunbar grinned. "Nothing, except that we're almost at High Rock."

"Already?"

"Already. Got your seat belts fastened? We're going down."

Jim checked his seat belt and once more turned to the window.

"I don't see Ron or Darlene down there," he said, "but it looks as though we're going to have plenty of company to watch us land."

The muscles in the pilot's face tightened. "Maybe we'll have company, and maybe not."

"What do you mean by that?"

The pilot did not answer.

In a moment or two Ernie spoke up. "Look down there. We're going to have company, all right. I'll bet everyone in the settlement has come out to meet the plane."

Mr. Dunbar laughed, but without humor. "Maybe they haven't seen who we are yet."

Jim's eyes widened. "That wouldn't make any difference, would it?"

"You wait and see."

He brought the plane around in a wide, sweeping arc to head into the slight wind. For perhaps half a minute the occupants in the little aircraft could not see the place where the Indians had gathered, their bright clothes standing out against the green of the forests. When they started their approach Jim caught his breath sharply.

"What's the matter?" Mr. Dunbar asked.

"Where is everybody?"

"They just saw who we are. That's all."

Jim turned to stare at him. "You're kidding, aren't you?"

They touched down.

"Look for yourself. They're gone."

"Does that always happen?"

He nodded cryptically. "That's right. They all come out until they see who we are. Then they disappear."

Jim scowled and ran his hand across his face. "Ron has mentioned a couple of times that it's been tough getting started up here, but I didn't have any idea he was having that sort of opposition."

"Saying it's tough here at High Rock is the understatement of the year."

The pilot slowed the aircraft to taxiing speed and headed toward the small docking area. When they were about a dozen yards out, he shut off the engine.

"Jim," he said, "will you get out on your float and help me paddle us ashore?"

"Sure thing."

The boy did as he was told. Moments later the float nosed into the sand and Jim jumped lightly to the beach.

"Want to tie her up?"

The pilot shook his head. "Nope. I think I'll be on my way as soon as you guys and your gear get ashore. I did plan on only making the one trip today, but now the early start will let me get back and get the other fellows in here tonight, too."

By this time Darlene Orlis was hurrying down the hill toward them. Her face lit up happily when she saw Jim. "Jim!" she cried.

She came up quickly and would have kissed him had he not ducked away and thrust out his hand.

"It's so good to see you, Jim!" she exclaimed again.

"It's good to see you, too."

For several minutes they were both talking at once. "How's everybody at home?" she asked at last.

"Just like they always are." He looked about. "Where's Ron? Isn't he here?"

"He went to one of the neighboring settlements to do some visiting."

Jim introduced her to Ernie. About that time the

pilot called from the plane. "Have you fellows got anything else in here?"

They looked around. "I guess not. I think we've got everything here on shore."

"If you'll give me a shove back into the water, I'll go back for your friends."

When he was gone the two boys picked up their gear and started up the narrow footpath with Darlene. She was still talking excitedly, asking about Danny and Kay, and Mr. and Mrs. Orlis and all the others she knew. Jim tried his best to answer her excited questions.

Halfway up the hill they met two youthful Crees who were apparently a little older than Jim. He smiled broadly as he spoke to them. Their eyes were cold and expressionless as they met his. Neither spoke. Jim stopped and turned to watch them until they rounded a bend in the path.

"What was the matter with them?" he asked. "Don't they speak English?"

Darlene's face grew serious and the happy gleam in her eyes dulled. "They speak English, all right," she said.

"You mean they're that unfriendly?"

In spite of herself, she shivered. "That's hardly the word for the way they seem to feel about us."

"But why?" he asked. "You've come here to help them. It doesn't seem that would make them so angry."

"I don't know for sure why they're so unfriendly," she went on. "Ron says that it's because they are so opposed to the gospel, but I don't know."

Ron Orlis returned to High Rock about the same time Mr. Dunbar flew in with Wade and Ray that afternoon. They all sat up until almost one o'clock in the morning talking about old times at CBI and about the work Ron had invited them to come up and do.

Finally, Ernie voiced the question that had been bothering the boys since they arrived and felt the hostility.

"This may not be very polite," he said, "but there's something I've got to ask you."

Ron smiled. "Ask away," he said.

"I've been wondering why you asked us to come up here and do some building when you've met such violent opposition to the gospel. Is it wise to continue to invest money in a place like this?"

There was a short silence.

"That's a fair question. To tell you the truth I've asked myself that same thing many times. And I'm sure the board members who decided on the building have had to do some serious heart-searching before reaching a decision."

"You must have a good reason for doing it."

"Actually, we do have," Ron continued. "I think we made the decision because of the opposition we've run into here at High Rock."

"That seems strange."

"We have an Indian evangelist and his wife who are willing to come up here and work in the settlement with us if we will provide them with a subsistence wage and a house to live in. The board felt that an Indian would have a much better response to his ministry than we would have."

Ron grinned. "I suppose you've already sensed that they don't trust Darlene and me very much."

"From what I've seen I'd say they don't trust any of us," Wade continued, "and they don't like us much, either."

The following morning after breakfast Ron took the fellows out to the place where they were going to build the cabin.

"The Indian who owned this ground wouldn't even let us use it for a white man's cabin," Ron explained. "He said that only another Indian could move onto his land."

"I didn't realize the feelings against the white man are as deep as that."

"That may not be the only thing. The white man hasn't treated the Indians well at all. They did just like we did in the States, although they made peace with the Indians early and didn't have the wars that we had when they came in and took the land." Ron's face grew dark. "And the white man has only brought corruption and ruin to the Indians for the most part. The white man's liquor and diseases have done the Indians a lot of harm. And, of course, the white man came in and began to take the lumber, the game, and the mineral resources. It's no wonder the Indians feel as they do about us."

"It's really a marvel that you're able to work at all," Wade continued.

Ron took a deep breath and slowly expelled it. "It's only through the grace of God that we're able to do anything here at High Rock."

* * *

That afternoon Jim went down to the trading post on an errand for Darlene. When he entered the building four or five young Indian men were standing in the back of the store laughing and talking in English.

"Just you wait!" one of them was saying. "One day we get Ron Orlis! We get him good!"

CHAPTER 3

INDIAN THREAT

The laughter of the Indian men filled the small trading post. For a brief instant Jim stood motionless, breathing heavily. Then, forgetting the things Darlene had sent him to get, he turned on his heel and hurried outside. He was in such a hurry that he almost ran into a couple of women who were approaching the store.

"Ex–excuse me!" he said.

He was panting hard when he burst into the living room of Ron and Darlene's simple little cabin.

"Ron!" he cried. "Ron!"

"He's not here, Jim." Darlene came out of the kitchen. "Did you get the salt and coffee I sent you for?"

Blankly he stared at her. "I–I was supposed to get something at the trading post for you, wasn't I?" He turned so she could not see the concern in his eyes.

"If that isn't just like a boy!" She laughed pleasantly.

"What does Kay do so you don't forget what she sends you after? Does she tie a string around your finger or send a note for the storekeeper?"

He grinned sheepishly. "You don't have to rub it in. I'll get your salt and coffee for you – just as soon as I get hold of Ron. I–I've got to see him about something. Is he still over at the place where we're going to make the building?"

"I think so," she replied. "He said there were some things he wanted to show the fellows before they start work tomorrow."

Jim made for the door. "Thanks."

"Don't forget to go to the trading post for me before you come back."

"Don't give it another thought. It's as good as done."

He dashed across the clearing toward the path that led to the site of the Indian evangelist's new cabin. About halfway there he met Ron and the others on their way back.

"Hold up a sec, fella," Ron said. "Where do you think you're going?"

Jim was panting so hard that he could scarcely speak. "Ron! I–I've got to talk to you!"

The young missionary grasped him by the arm. "What's the matter, Jim? What's wrong?"

Jim continued to pull in his breath in long, painful gasps.

"What is it?" Ron's voice raised. "Is Darlene all right?"

"It's nothing like that." He straightened forcibly until his gaze met Ron's. "I–I went down to the trading post for her a little while ago and–and while I was there, I heard these guys talking and–" His voice broke.

"Yes?"

"They–they're going to do something terrible to you, Ron," he said.

Ron Orlis sighed his relief. "Oh, is that all!"

"But you don't understand! There were half a dozen of them and they've really got it in for you. They were all bragging about what they're going to do to you when they catch you."

Ron would have gone on up the path without discussing the matter further, but Ernie stopped him.

"Wait a minute, Ron," he said. "I don't think you're putting enough importance on this. I saw how those fellows disappeared yesterday when they realized it was the mission plane coming in, and I saw them glaring at us when we met a couple of them on the path up to your cabin. There's a lot of real hatred in the hearts of some of the people here."

The others nodded solemnly.

"You don't know what guys like that would do to you, if they got the chance," Wade replied.

Ron stopped and slowly turned to face them.

"I appreciate your concern, fellows," he said, "and I do know what the situation is. Believe me. And I am concerned about it. But I've got to confess that this doesn't shake me up too much. Where did all of this take place, Jim?"

"In the trading post," he said. "I went in to get some things for Darlene and there were all these guys standing in the back of the store. They were all talking about you, Ron, and it wasn't good. I tell you, they're bad medicine."

Ron's grin widened.

"All of this talk was in English, wasn't it?"

"Oh, sure. I couldn't have understood them if they hadn't spoken in English."

"Doesn't it seem a little strange to you that they were talking about 'getting me' in English where both you and the Hudson Bay manager could hear?"

Jim's forehead crinkled.

"I–I don't know. I hadn't thought of that."

"I've got a hunch they were only giving you the 'business,' Jim. I think they saw you coming and thought it would be a good chance to let you overhear them and get you good and scared."

"It could be," he said, his reluctance to believe apparent in his voice.

"And he might have thought it would be a good chance for them to get me scared, too."

Jim thought it over momentarily.

"I suppose you could be right," he acknowledged. "But, they sure did sound mad at you."

Ron nodded in understanding.

"Oh, they dislike me enough to make them want to do a lot of things to try and scare us out. And they probably meant what they said about wanting to 'get' me, as they put it. But I don't think they'd be advertising it if they actually planned on trying anything very drastic."

Wade spoke up. "That could be, but I'd watch my step if I were you. I wouldn't take any chances."

Jim nodded. "That's exactly the way I feel about it." He shivered nervously. "If I were in your boots, I wouldn't want to meet those guys on a dark night. I can tell you that much."

Ron started for his cabin. "It's not going to do us any good to stand here and talk about them," he went on, "or even concern ourselves about them. We've got other things to do."

Nothing more was said until they were all sitting at the dinner table that noon. Darlene began to question Jim.

"I've been doing a lot of thinking about you the last hour or so, Jim," she said. "It wasn't like you to forget my packages at the trading post. It wasn't like you at all."

Color crept into his cheeks, but he said nothing.

"What was it all about, anyway?"

There was no answer.

"Jim Morgan," she said, "you're keeping something from me."

He looked up sheepishly.

"What makes you think that?"

"I know you too well. Now, start at the beginning and tell me exactly what this is all about."

His gaze met Ron's.

"Darlene," Ron said, "I asked Jim not to say

anything to you about this because I didn't want to worry you. He overheard some fellows talking about me in the Bay store and got all shook up."

Her face went ashen. "I thought it must be something like that."

"But it's nothing to be so concerned about," Ron persisted. "They were just trying to scare Jim."

She spoke hesitantly. "Are you sure?"

"Of course, I'm sure. You know how the young fellows are around here, don't you?"

"Yes, I know how they are. That's just the trouble. I know exactly how they are."

It was some time before Jim spoke again. "I don't understand it, Ron. Why would the people be so angry with you when you're only here to try to help them?"

The missionary's smile was fleeting. "I suppose the main reason they don't like us is that we're preaching salvation to them," he said. "And as they hear us, they're beginning to feel that they're sinners. I suppose they're even afraid that they might make a decision for Christ. And they've heard enough to know that if that happens, they'll have to change their ways. So, they get angry with us."

Darlene sighed deeply. "There are times when I find myself listening to Satan when he tells me that it isn't worth it for us to stay here."

"Don't say that," Ron said quickly. "Don't ever think it! This is where God has called us to serve Him. It's the only place for us to be."

* * *

Ron had hoped to have some logs cut for the cabin the boys were going to help him build so they could start work immediately without losing any time. However, he had not been able to get any of the Indians to work for him. He had done what he could alone, but he only had about half enough cut and peeled by the time the boys from CBI and Jim got there.

"I suppose the first thing we've got to do is to find some cedar logs."

Wade spoke quickly. "Why don't we go out and cut down some trees? That wouldn't take long."

"We might have to do that," Ron said, "but I don't want to unless we absolutely have to. Green logs will warp and twist out of shape as they dry. You can't build a very good cabin with them."

Jim joined in. "Why don't you do what Uncle Carl used to do, Ron?" he asked. "When he needed dry logs and didn't have any, he found someone who had some dry ones they weren't going to use for a while and traded them for green logs."

"I'd thought of that." Ron went over and sat down wearily on a deadfall. "There are plenty of fellows with poles cut. But I don't think any of them would let us have them." He let out his breath slowly. "I did hear yesterday that there's a white trapper across the lake who has some cedar poles cut and piled. It'll be quite a job getting them over here, but I believe it'd be worth the effort."

Wade nodded in agreement. "Why don't you see about getting the logs?" he said. "We'll finish the clearing and get some posts set to lay the stringers on."

Jim eyed Ron curiously.

"What gives with these people, Ron?" he asked. "Why do they have such a hatred for the gospel?"

The youthful missionary smiled. "I wondered about that for a long time myself. I told you about the way they've been treated by the white man in the past. Well, it's still going on."

"What do you mean?"

"A fisheries company came up here," Ron continued, "made a contract with the people, and then proceeded to cheat them terribly."

"A Christian company did that?"

Ron shook his head. "No, the company was far from Christian. But in the eyes of the people Christianity is the white man's religion and the fisheries was a white man's company. Therefore, they blamed Christianity for what had happened to them and determined that they are going to have nothing to do with it."

"That's hardly fair."

"No, it isn't fair at all. But I can understand why they feel that way." He sighed wearily. "Our responsibility is to live before them in such a way that they'll see that there is a big difference."

That afternoon Ron took his motor-powered boat across High Rock Lake and made arrangements to get logs from the white trapper.

"You'll have to tow them across," he said, "but you're sure welcome to them if you want them. I don't have any use for them."

"I really appreciate that," Ron said. "We'll come over and cut green logs for you to replace these."

"You don't need to bother," the trapper replied. "You see, I met a woman in Saskatoon when I was there a couple of years ago. We was doin' some serious talkin' about gettin' hitched and I figgered I'd need me a bigger cabin. 'Fore I got around to gettin' the cabin built she up an' married some guy across the street, so I was stuck with them cedar logs."

"That was too bad."

"Oh, it coulda been worse," he went on. "It coulda happened after I had the cabin built."

On the way back home, Ron stopped at the Hudson Bay Trading Post. As he started home again, he met a dozen young men clustered on the path between the store and his place.

"Hello, fellows," he said as warmly as possible.

They glared at him. When he had almost reached them, one young man about his size stepped directly into the path to block his way.

"Where do you think you're goin'?" he asked, his voice taunting.

Ron felt the color rise in his cheeks. He stopped momentarily.

CHAPTER 4

BOLD ENCOUNTER

For an instant or two Ron was startled. This was no chance meeting. It was planned – the thing the Indians had been talking about when they allowed Jim to overhear them. They were doing this deliberately in an attempt to provoke a fight.

But he couldn't fight. That was out of the question. In the first place, the instant he made a move toward the young man who was taunting him, the others would pile in to give him a beating. But more important, if he ever hit one of them, regardless of the provocation, he and Darlene might as well move. Their chances of being a testimony and reaching anyone for Christ would be gone.

The Indian boy shoved forward belligerently.

"Where you think you going?" he demanded.

"Step aside, please." There was no anger in either Ron's voice or eyes. Only unswerving determination.

The blustering Indian faltered momentarily in the face of Ron's show of firmness. The missionary caught the flicker of fear and uncertainty in his eyes.

"I said, step aside!" he repeated quietly.

"Who's goin' to make me?" He glanced at his companions on one side and then the other. And when he spoke again, his voice grew bolder. "Who's goin' to make me?" he repeated. "That's what I want for to know. Who make me step aside?"

With an unspoken prayer in his heart, Ron stepped forward. His movements were slow and calculated so there was no mistaking his intentions. Surprise gleamed in the Cree's eyes. Surprise and indecision. Apparently, this was something he hadn't expected.

The Indian boy could cope with a fight one way or the other. And he could deal with outright retreat. But this was neither. Ron Orlis simply moved ahead without haste or fear, as though he were completely confident that he would not be challenged. There was a brief twinkling of hesitation – of doubt. Then the Indian retreated reluctantly by half a step.

Ron resisted the impulse to hurry by, but neither did he linger.

"Thank you," he said quietly.

Without breaking stride, he moved past them. The boys stared at him, mouths gaping.

* * *

At the supper table that evening Ron started to say something to Jim and his companions about what had happened, but he changed his mind. It was not until everyone else had turned in and he and Darlene were alone that he told her what had taken place.

Fear leaped to her eyes as he told the story.

"Oh, Ron!"

He laughed. "Now, Darlene. Don't let yourself get all shaken up about it. Nothing really happened. They just thought they could bluff me into turning around but found that they couldn't. That was all." He sat down and pulled off his shoes. "Something like this was bound to happen sooner or later. It's been building up for weeks."

"I'm not so concerned about what happened today," she told him. "That's over and done with. What I'm concerned about is what's going to happen next."

"We're in a better position now to avoid trouble than we've ever been before," he said. "They know now that they can't bluff me."

She went to the window and nervously adjusted the shade.

"I wish I could think that it's all over now, Ron," she said, "but I can't. I'm afraid that it's just beginning."

He reached over and tenderly took her by the hand.

"We can't let it get us, Darlene," he said quietly. "We're here to do a job for the Lord. If we weaken and quit, we're playing right into Satan's hands."

She nodded her understanding. "I know, Ron. But

I know their bitterness and hatred toward us, and I can't help being disturbed."

Ron was a long while in answering. "When they take Christ as their Savior they won't be bitter, nor will they hate us. We can never lose sight of that."

For the next several days Ron did not see the Indian fellows again. In fact, it was so quiet that he all but forgot the incident on the path. While the fellows on the work crew carried the logs down to the lake and towed them over to the building site, he started calling on homes once more.

On his way home after an afternoon of visiting he met two of the same young men on the path. The instant he saw them his lithe body tensed. He cautiously judged their mood. They were sneering at him, but their belligerence seemed to be gone.

"Hi," he said.

They stood to one side, but it was obvious that they wanted to talk to him.

"Where you go?"

"Home." He spoke quietly, but there was strength and boldness in his voice.

The Indians turned toward each other, grinning crookedly.

"Shall we tell him?"

His companion frowned.

"We tell him and he get scared. Better we say nothing."

"We tell him so he can run and hide, eh?"

Slowly their smiles disappeared.

"You make fun of us," one of them said. "You much big *Okimaw* [Boss]. Big deal!" His lips curled around the words in a bitter snarl. "You think you tough!"

Ron contradicted him. "That's where you're wrong. I've never considered myself tough, at all."

The taller Indian laughed raucously.

"Maybe you already hear about Guy Ferebee? Maybe you know what he do to you?"

Ron's face twisted curiously. "Who's Guy Ferebee?"

"You never hear of Guy Ferebee?"

"I can't say that I have."

"You will." The snarl twisted into a derisive laugh. "You hear much about him. You meet him, maybe. You feel his fist!" Threateningly he held up his own fist and shook it.

"Maybe you'd better tell me what this is all about." The muscles in the missionary's face tightened. "I've never met nor even heard of this Guy Ferebee, whoever he is. Why would he want to fight with me?"

The Indian took half a step closer and leaned forward, his voice lowering.

"He no like preachers. He say he run first preacher who come to High Rock out of settlement."

"That's interesting. And where's he been all the time we've lived here? Why hasn't he come to see us before?"

"He work by Hay River," the spokesman explained. "He in Territories. But he come back." The Cree's voice raised threateningly. "He beat you 'til you go out of High Rock and never come back."

Ron laughed as though it were some sort of a joke that they had told him. The Indian boys seemed disappointed.

"You wait!" they warned. "You wait!"

"I'll tell you what you do," Ron said. "When this friend of yours comes around, have him look me up. I'd like to talk to him."

The next few days Ron wasn't the only one who heard about Guy Ferebee. Everywhere Jim and his friends went they were taunted by the news.

"You ready for leave?" one of the Cree lads asked Jim.

"Not so you could notice. We're not going home 'til school starts. We've got a job to do here."

"Guy Ferebee, he see about that." The Indian boy grinned evilly. "He give preacher good beating. Then you all leave."

"You'd better not count on it," Jim told him.

But, in spite of his bravado, Jim was still quite concerned. He tried to talk with Ron about it, but that was useless. Ron refused to listen.

"They want to get us scared more than anything else," he said. "And if they can succeed in doing that, they've already won half the battle."

"But–"

"Forget it, Jim, and get back to work. There's nothing we can accomplish by getting all worked up about it. All we can do is stay on the job and trust the Lord to work it all out."

Reluctantly the Morgan boy did as he was told.

That night while Ron and the CBI students were

playing caroms in the living room, Jim went out into the kitchen and talked to Darlene.

"I'm worried about what those guys might do to Ron, Darlene," he said, keeping his voice down.

She hung the dish towel on the rack.

"He won't fight this Indian, Jim," she said firmly.

"Oh yes he will," Jim retorted. "He'll have to fight him. Those Indian guys'll see to that. They're going to get this Guy Ferebee and Ron together and make him fight. He won't be able to help himself."

"Humanly speaking, I suppose that's true," she went on. "But, Jim, we don't have to depend on our own strength. We've placed the matter in God's hands, and we're trusting Him to take care of everything."

Doubtfully the boy shook his head.

"I suppose what you're saying is true," he said, "but this is one time I don't see how everything's going to work out."

* * *

Guy Ferebee did not arrive when he was supposed to, but he was on the floatplane that came in from the north on Tuesday afternoon. Ron happened to be in the Hudson Bay store at the time. He hadn't finished buying his groceries when the front door flung open and an Indian boy fourteen or fifteen years old came running in.

"Guy Ferebee is here!" he cried. "He's on his way over here right now!"

Ron did not look up.

"I'll take these items with me, Joe," he said to the Bay Company manager, "but I think I'll have the fellows come with me to carry the rest of this stuff."

"Suits me. I'll put it up for you and you can get it anytime you want it." The older white man lowered his voice to a hoarse whisper. "You'd better duck out the back door while you've got a chance to get away."

"No thanks."

"You don't know this Guy Ferebee. He's as big as a grizzly bear and twice as mean. He'll tear you apart."

"Maybe," Ron answered, "but I can't run from him. If I do, I'm finished here in High Rock."

"If you don't, you might be finished in High Rock in an entirely different way. Did anyone ever tell you why he hasn't been here until now?"

Ron shook his head.

"He's been in jail for assaulting some guy he'd never seen before."

Ron's lips parted as though to speak, but before he had the opportunity to do so the door opened and a burly giant of a man filled the opening. He was lean and youthful, and his eyes flamed angrily. Half a dozen young Crees about his own age pushed close behind him.

He stood there, arms hanging loosely at his sides, while his eyes swept the trading post. At last, they came to rest on Ron.

"You!" His voice was ice. "Are you the preacher?"

CHAPTER 5

A SACK OF FLOUR

For as long as a minute Guy Ferebee stared at Ron. "Are you the preacher?" He shot out the question once more.

"That's right." Ron was as quiet and emotionless as though he had been asked the time of day. "I'm a minister of the gospel," he said, "and a missionary to High Rock."

Deliberately the towering Cree stepped forward. In silence his friends pushed through the door behind him.

"Did anybody tell you I say I run any preacher away who come to High Rock?"

The young missionary smiled faintly. "Come to think of it, some of your friends did tell me something like that."

"What are you? Smart guy?" He took another step forward and whipped off his heavy wool sweater.

"Oh no you don't," the store manager broke in quickly. "There's not going to be any fighting in my store."

Cold rage glittered in the Indian's dark eyes.

"Who stop me?"

"If nobody else can, I'll call the Mounties on the radio. They'll fly in here and have you back in town and locked up before the day's out." He came around the corner of the long counter. "Now turn around and get out of here."

Ferebee hesitated.

"You'll be wanting credit before the next trapping season," the manager continued. "But if you start a fight in here you'll not get a pound of supplies without cash. Is that clear?"

Guy Ferebee took another step forward hesitantly. Losing credit was something he hadn't considered. That was enough to make him stop and think. A man had to have credit in case his luck went bad.

"Come outside, Preacher." His anger seemed even more intent. "You come outside or I take you out!"

Ron remained motionless. The manager of the Hudson Bay store came up beside him.

"Just stay in here and you'll be all right. He's afraid to tackle you as long as you're in here. He won't want to lose his credit."

The huge Indian's fist was working belligerently. "What is the matter? Afraid your God no protect you?"

Without any sign of fear the young missionary let his gaze meet the Cree's. An unspoken prayer welled up in his heart.

He moved forward quietly until he was standing beside the stack of hundred-pound sacks of flour that were common in that part of the north.

"What does flour weigh today, Joe?" he asked.

"The same as it did yesterday," the Hudson Bay manager snorted.

With that Ron grasped the heavy sack with his hand, lifted it a foot off the pile, and hoisted it at arm's length above his head.

The big Indian stared, surprised momentarily at the ease with which Ron handled the big sack. His body relaxed slightly.

"Here!" Ron spoke sharply. "Catch!"

With that he threw the sack of flour to the big Cree. Almost involuntarily the Indian threw up his hands to catch it. It caught him off guard and he staggered backward, almost falling under the weight of it. He held it briefly. Then his fingers relaxed and he let it slide down his legs to the floor. A strange, perplexed look twisted his face.

The Indians clustered behind Ferebee were eyeing Ron in silence. Although they did not speak, something akin to respect glittered in their dark eyes.

The big fellow was still standing there gasping for breath when Ron went up to him, stooped and picked up the sack of flour as easily as he had a moment before.

"If you get a hankering to play games, Guy," he said, "come on up anytime."

* * *

Ron said nothing to the others about his encounter with Guy Ferebee, but the story soon spread around the settlement. Jim heard it the next day and went racing to Ron to learn the rest of the account in detail.

"I'd like to have been there!" he exclaimed, grinning broadly. "Oh, I'd have liked to have been there. Joe at the store told me he thought that ugly bruiser was going to take you apart."

Ron laughed. "Let me clue you in. Joe wasn't the only one who was doing some tall thinking. And that's not all. I was praying plenty, too."

"You know what else Joe said?" Jim continued. "He said his eyes about popped out of his head when you picked up that sack of flour the way you did. He said he'd never seen anything like that before. And from the surprised look on Guy Ferebee's face, he hadn't either. He said Ferebee figured he was lucky to get out of that deal OK."

Ron picked up a little twig and broke it in two.

"I'll let you in on a secret," he said. "You know where I worked the last two years I went to school? At a big potato warehouse in Cedarton. All I did almost every afternoon was lug one-hundred-pound sacks of potatoes around. I learned how to handle them, let me tell you."

But Jim would not let him explain it away so easily. "You can try to make it sound as though there wasn't anything to it if you want to, but you can't fool me. I know better. There isn't one guy in a thousand who could do what you did in the Hudson Bay store yesterday."

Ron laughed. "If you keep that up, you'll give me a big head."

"It's not just me. It's Joe and everyone else who hears about it. I don't think you'll have any more trouble with that Ferebee character."

A strange look crossed the missionary's face. "I wish I could be as sure of it as you are." His voice grew even more serious. "I'm afraid this is only the beginning. A fellow like Ferebee isn't going to quit that easily. He hates the gospel and is going to do everything he can to stop it."

"Anyway," Jim continued, "you're over the first hurdle."

Ron nodded. "Yes," he said thoughtfully. "And we can thank God for answering our prayers."

Jim and the CBI students had been working hard on the cabin at High Rock for two full weeks. They hadn't had an opportunity to go fishing on the lake until Ron insisted that they take some time off.

"Tomorrow's Friday," he said. "I want you to take tomorrow and the next day and do some fishing. Take a tent if you want to and stay all night on one of the islands."

Wade's entire being lighted up. "You don't have to suggest that again, as far as I'm concerned. I've hardly been able to stand looking at the lake, I've been so anxious to get out there fishing."

Jim had been planning to go along, but at the last minute he changed his mind. He and Ron helped them get their gear together and carried it down to the lake. On the way back to the cabin after the fishermen left, Ron put his arm affectionately around Jim's shoulders.

"I'm sure glad you stuck around tonight, Jim. We haven't had much time to spend alone since you got here."

"That's what I was figuring," Jim said. "And besides, I–I didn't want to leave you alone with that Ferebee character around."

"We were going to forget about Ferebee. Remember?"

"I wish it were that easy."

They sat around the supper table that night, talking a little later than usual. It was almost midnight when they finally went to bed.

The discordant beat of drums and weird chanting drifted through the open window. Jim stood beside his bed, listening. It must be one of those dances Ron had been telling him about. Shivers tingled icily up his spine. He crawled into bed and tried to blot it out of his hearing. At last, he drifted off to sleep.

How long he had been sleeping he did not know, but it must have been the middle of the night when he was awakened by a sound in the other room.

At first, he stirred dreamily, conscious only of the fact that he had heard something. He rolled over on his side when the sound came again.

This time he was awake instantly. He jerked bolt upright in bed! Somebody had stumbled into a kitchen chair.

Then Ron's voice sounded in the still night air. "Who's there?"

Jim's blood froze.

Guy Ferebee! He was the only one in the village who would dare to come into Ron and Darlene's cabin at night! And he was probably drunk!

What could Ron do now?

CHAPTER 6

NIGHT INTRUDER

Jim's breath was coming in short, quick stabs. Those Indians actually had meant what they said about "getting" Ron! He tried to get out of bed, but fear momentarily stole the strength from his legs and numbed his mind.

At that moment he heard the other bedroom door open and Ron called out sternly, "Who's there?"

"It–it only me – Charlie One Bear." The voice was old and quavering.

"What do you want, Charlie?" Ron asked.

There was no answer.

"It's almost one o'clock. You should be home in bed."

By this time Jim had jumped out of bed and tip-toed quietly to the door. Ron lit the gas lamp, and the white glare revealed a wrinkled, gray haired old man.

"You shouldn't be out at this hour," Ron said once more.

"I–I afraid for go home."

"You're afraid to go home? Why?"

Fear flickered in the old man's dark eyes. "I am fear of what they do. They come to my house. Eat all our food. They chase me away. They scare my wife and our–our grandchildren. I am fear to go home."

Through the crack in the door Jim saw the muscles in Ron's face tighten. "Who did this to you?" he asked. "Who came into your house and drove you away?"

The old man struggled desperately with the words. "The young men. Drink much. Come my house." He seemed to shudder.

Ron breathed deeply. "What do you want me to do?"

"I am fear for go home."

"But you can't stay here. Your wife and your grand-children need you. They'll be worried about what's happened to you. You'll have to go back."

The Indian man hesitated. "You go with me. Then I–I no be afraid."

Ron nodded. "I'll go with you."

Darlene, who had slipped into a robe and joined her husband and their uninvited visitor in the kitchen, spoke up. "Oh, no."

Her youthful husband turned to her. "We can't let those drunken young fellows terrorize this poor man and his wife, Darlene. I've got to walk over there with him."

Concern gleamed in her eyes. "Don't you see, Ron?" she echoed. "This is just a trap. They want to get you out alone at night so they can give you a beating."

He kissed her lightly. "Don't get so shook up, Honey. I'm not afraid of them."

"I'd feel a little better if you were."

Numbly, Darlene watched Ron and Charlie One Bear leave the cabin. She was still rooted to the middle of the floor when Jim joined her.

"Do–do you really think this is a trap to get Ron over to that old man's house?" he asked fearfully.

"It could be."

"Maybe I'd better go along."

"He wouldn't let you."

"But he doesn't have to know anything about it."

"What could you do, Jim?" she asked him thoughtfully.

"I could follow along behind and run for you or the Hudson Bay man if they should try to beat up on Ron," he said.

She walked nervously to the door and stared out into the darkness. "At least I'd know if something happened to him," she said, her voice quavering.

Jim took her statement for agreement and got into his clothes quickly. A prayer welled up in his heart as he hurried down the path. There was no know-ing what would happen when Ron got to Charlie's cabin – if the drunken men had waited that long. They might even waylay him on the path. And by the time Jim got back with help they could have broken every bone in Ron's body! He shivered and hurried a little faster.

Ron and Charlie were up the path two or three hundred yards ahead of Jim. The young missionary glanced speculatively at his companion.

Darlene could very well be right. The fellows might have tricked old Charlie into getting him out of the house and over to Ron and Darlene's that night, or they might have let him in on the deal himself. His fear seemed genuine enough, though. If he was putting on, he was a better actor than Ron had thought. Moistening his lips with the tip of his tongue, Ron prayed again silently.

Not far ahead he could hear the voices of the young men. Charlie stopped and squeezed Ron's arm convulsively.

"They out here now," he said. "They come after Charlie!"

But Ron did not slacken his pace.

"Come on," he said in a guarded whisper. "We've got as much right to be on this path as they have."

Soon they were close enough so Ron could make out four or five shadowy forms on the path ahead. It was obvious from their loud voices that they had been drinking.

In a moment they recognized the missionary.

"Look who come to our party. Where you going so late, Preacher?"

One of the others spoke. "You no scared of dark, eh?"

Ron did not raise his voice. "Step aside, please." He continued to walk toward them. Old Charlie was half trotting to keep up with him.

Ron's lack of fear and indecision seemed to unnerve

the drunken men. They fell back silently, allowing him and his Indian companion to pass.

Jim, who had been following along behind, ducked into the brush and avoided the group of men. By the time he reached the One Bear cabin Ron and Charlie were on the porch. The old Indian spoke plaintively. "You–you go in first. I'll wait out here."

But Ron opened the door and half-thrust the gray-haired Cree in ahead of him. There were five or six young Indians in the room, laughing and talking boisterously. The old man's wife and grandchildren were huddled together in a corner, eyes dark with fear.

As the intruders saw Ron and Charlie, they fell silent. One of them spoke belligerently.

"What you want?" Hatred curled his lips.

"Charlie doesn't want you in his house," he said. "You're frightening his wife and grandchildren. You'll have to leave."

The Indian's voice rose to a crescendo.

"S'pose we no want for leave!" Drink slurred his words. "What you do then?"

Ron did not reply. Instead, he reached out, grasped the tall young Cree firmly by the wrist, and jerked him toward the door.

"Now, get out and don't come back." He spoke decisively. "And the rest of you, go with him and don't come back here. You know what your chief will do if he finds out you've been out here terrorizing Charlie and his wife tonight."

Silently the Indians did as they were told. All except Guy Ferebee. The big, hulking Cree was still sitting at the table, a whole ham before him. He had been cutting thick slices of the meat with the knife in his hand and had been eating it cold.

Now his gaze met Ron's.

"I said you were to leave." Ron spoke with renewed firmness.

A sneer twisted Guy's face.

"I no feel like go. Now what you think of that?"

Ron's fixed gaze met his. Then, without warning, the missionary leaped forward and grasped the hulking intruder by the shoulder.

"I said for you to leave." He jerked the surprised young Indian to his feet. "Now, get out of this house and stay out."

Before either Ron or Guy quite realized what was happening the missionary guided him to the door and shoved him outside.

"Now I want all of you out there to know this!" Ron raised his voice so that the others who had been in the cabin would be sure to hear him. "You're not going to come over here and bother Charlie and his family again! If you do, you'll have to answer to me and your chief."

Guy slunk off into the darkness.

* * *

Ernie and the rest of the CBI crew came back to High Rock the following afternoon with half a dozen large lake trout and stories of fabulous fishing.

"You never saw anything like it, Jim," he said. "You should've been along."

"You should've been here," the Morgan boy said. "We could've used you last night." He told them everything that had taken place.

When he finished the other boys sat in silence until at last, Ernie spoke. "I wonder if that's the end of it."

"I thought it would be," Jim said. "I told Ron I didn't think they'd dare to bother him again after the way he stood up to them and they backed down. But he doesn't think they're going to give up so easily. He's got a hunch they'll try something else."

"So do I."

* * *

The following day was Sunday and nothing happened at all. In fact, it was so quiet and peaceful that the fellows all but forgot there had been any trouble with the young men at the settlement. They were working on the cabin Monday afternoon when Guy came striding up.

Ron saw him first and went to meet him.

"*Waaci,*" he said, greeting the young man as warmly as he could.

Guy did not reply for a moment. Hatred mingled

with the anger in his dark eyes. "I come to tell you you have to go."

Ron stared at him incredulously. "What do you mean?"

The Cree's voice grew loud and insulting. "Your cabin on my land. You move him! Get him off! Now!"

Ron could scarcely believe what he was hearing. "But I talked with your father," he said. "He told me that I could build here."

"This place for Indian. Your house on my land! You move!"

"But I got permission to build our cabin where it is, too. I did that before I cut a stick of timber or laid a log in place."

Guy's expression did not change. "You have paper that say you put cabin on land, eh?"

Ron felt the muscles in his stomach knot. "Your father gave me his word."

"You lie! Nobody say you can build on my land."

For a minute or two Ron stood there, staring blankly up at the big Indian who remained motionless before him.

"I don't mean to contradict you, Guy, but there's a terrible mistake somewhere. I got permission from your father to put our house where it is. Before I even talked with him about it, I went to the chief and got his permission, too."

"The chief have nothing for do with our land," Guy said doggedly.

"I know that, but I wanted to be sure that it was all right for us to build here. I didn't want to have any trouble about it."

The towering Cree's lips twisted into a thin snarl. "White man lie!" He spat out the words and then turned haughtily and strode away.

Jim and the others who had been listening breathlessly to the exchange, clustered about him.

"Now, what was that all about?" the younger boy wanted to know.

Ron tried to grin feebly. He knew his face was ashen and moist with perspiration.

"What's he trying to pull?" Jim asked.

"Something I never thought that he'd dare to do. He says that we've got to move our house. He says the land it's on is his and neither he nor his father gave permission for us to build where we did."

Jim was furious. "The big lug just wants to cause trouble!" he exploded. "He can't do that!"

Ron was silent for a brief space of time.

"Frankly," he said, "I don't know for sure what he can do and what he can't."

"Didn't you say that the land belongs to his dad?" Jim persisted.

"The land's his dad's, all right," he said, nodding. "I checked on that. But Guy might figure that it's going to be his someday, so he's got the right to say what can and what can't be done with it."

"Then all you've got to do is go and talk to his

dad," Jim said. "He listened to you once. If you go over the thing, he'll listen to you again."

"I wish I could be as sure of that as you are. These people hang together better than a lot of others. He acted as though he already had permission from his father to do whatever he wants to do with the ground."

Jim picked up a stick and broke it in two, impulsively. "The crazy guys! They won't even recognize that you're only here to help them. Couldn't you move into this cabin we're building now?"

Ron shook his head.

"Not a chance. You heard him say that this cabin is all right where it is because another Indian's going to live in it, didn't you?"

Ernie spoke up. "What do you think you'll have to do, Ron?" he asked.

The missionary shrugged his shoulders. "The way I see it we'll probably have to move."

"If you've got to move the cabin, we'll help you. It won't take long."

Ron sighed his deep concern. "Moving it isn't the biggest problem we've got by a long shot," he replied. "It won't take very long for a group of us to move it, that's true. But we've got to get permission to put it somewhere else. And now that this has happened, I don't know whether we'll be able to find anyone who'll let us have our cabin on his land or not."

Jim scowled. "I still don't get it," he said. "A fella comes all the way out here to help these people find

Christ as their Savior, and they get so mad at him that they want to run him out of the settlement."

"It isn't just the people here at High Rock who do things like that," Ron reminded him. "Even wealthy, well-educated men will get furious if they're approached for Christ. Their hatred is for Him, not Darlene and me." He picked up his hammer and handed it to Jim. "Take this back to the toolbox for me, will you? I think I'll go over and see old Mr. Ferebee. Maybe he'll be more agreeable to talk with than his son."

Ron found the old man sitting in the sun near his big lake. The old Indian only grunted in reply to his greeting.

"*Waaci.*"

"*Waaci.*"

"I've come to talk with you about something, Mr. Ferebee," Ron continued.

Cold, watery black eyes met his. "Talk."

"You gave me permission to build my cabin on your property, didn't you?"

Ferebee's eyes gleamed warily. "Who say I no give you permission for build on my land?"

"Your son was talking to me about it a little while ago," Ron went on. "He had the idea that I had built there without permission from you."

There was a short silence. "My son, he no like it you have cabin on my land," he said.

"But you gave permission."

The old man's face grew granite hard. "I give nothing!"

Ron stared at him in disbelief. "But–"

"I give nothing!" The old Indian's voice raised. "My son say you are for move. You move!"

Ron tried to reason with him. He recalled every phase of the discussion that had taken place the day he received permission to build on the Ferebee property. Finally, he pleaded with the elderly Cree. But it was useless. The wrinkled old Indian turned his back and refused to listen. At last, seeing that talking was hopeless, he walked away.

CHAPTER 7

FOUR DAYS TO MOVE

When Ron reached the cabin Darlene was waiting breathlessly for him, concern flickering in her eyes.

"Ron, what did Mr. Ferebee have to say?" she asked, her voice taut.

"Nothing." He crossed the floor and sat down heavily in a chair near the kitchen window. "Nothing very much. He just informed me that we've got to move our cabin!"

She gasped. "Ron!"

"That's right. We've got to move it."

"But you got permission to build here," she countered.

"Yes, we got permission," he said. "But when I saw him a little while ago, he swore that he didn't give us permission. He said that we had never talked about it with him – so we'll have to move."

She sank into a chair across from him. For a brief time her face was ashen and lifeless. "I don't see why we have to move our cabin when he told us we could build it here. It's just spite. He doesn't have any use for the land. He only wants to make it so hard for us that we'll have to move. I don't see why we have to take that kind of treatment."

Ron Orlis thought for a time. "I did talk with the Indian agent about it. I'm not sure whether he went to see Ferebee about it before we started to build or not. It might help for me to go and see him."

For a long while they looked at each other in silence.

"Do you think it would be wise to go and talk with the Indian agent?" she asked quietly.

"What do you mean?"

"I was just wondering about the way the other Indians might take it."

"I don't like to be shoved around," he said more to himself than to Darlene.

"None of us like to be shoved around," she said. "And when I think about what the Ferebees are doing to us I get so upset – and so angry that I feel as though I'd like to do something almost as bad to them just to get even. But I know that isn't the way to look at it. Even if we should be able to brave our way through and leave the cabin where it is now, we might be the losers in the long run."

Before Ron could answer she spoke again. "We might make enemies that it would take years for us to win back."

Ron thrust his fingers through his hair. "I suppose there's a lot of truth in that," he said. "But how much should we have to take before we fight back?"

There was a long silence. "How much did Christ take, Ron?"

She spoke quietly, but her words knifed into his heart. His gaze met hers, thoughtfully.

"I know that what you're saying is true, Darlene," he answered, "but it's sure not easy." His discouragement leaked through. "Sometimes I wonder whether it's even worth the effort for us to stay here and try to work among these people."

She crossed the floor and stood beside him, tangling her fingers in his hair. "Don't say that," she said. "Of course it's worthwhile."

He looked up. "Just exactly what have we accomplished?" he asked almost belligerently. "We can't hold services. We can't get anyone out to Bible study in our home, and nobody will let us come to their home for Bible study. There aren't more than two or three places in the whole settlement where we're welcome. When we go out visiting we are met in the yard and that's where we have to talk to them. Yet, we're taking money from the Lord's people so we can stay here. Is there any way of justifying that?"

She nodded, a smile lighting up her face. "Don't you remember the story you told me about the Art Wellwoods?" she asked. "They worked here in Saskatchewan at another hard station for eight solid years without a convert until Tommy and Helen Francis came along. They were won for Christ, went through Indian Bible school in Minnesota and became evangelists for the mission. They've won hundreds of their own people for Christ."

Ron's fingers sought hers and squeezed them lovingly.

"You couldn't say that the ministry of the Wellwoods was useless, could you?"

He shook his head.

"Maybe God has a Tommy Francis for us here at High Rock. Maybe that's why we're here."

A smile lit up his youthful face. "I'm sorry for getting so discouraged," he said, sighing deeply. "I know how hard it is to work here in the north. And I know the disappointments are many. But somehow, when a fellow talks about a work being hard, it doesn't actually register the way it does when he experiences it."

He laughed at himself with new understanding. "I think I had the idea that it was going to be different with you and me. I think I felt that we weren't going to have to wait years for converts the way some of the others have had to do. It was a real jolt to find out that our ministry is going to be as slow and as difficult as that of many of the other missionaries."

Darlene went back to the table and sat down. "What are you going to do about Guy Ferebee and his father?" she asked.

"I don't know for sure." He took a deep breath. "I think I'll go back and talk with him tomorrow and see if I can get him to change his mind. If I can't, I'll probably tell him that we'll move the cabin just as soon as we can."

"I'm glad you've decided to do that, Ron," she said. "I think it's the only way."

The following morning he left the house as soon as they had finished breakfast and went over to see the tall young Cree. Guy wasn't at home and he had difficulty locating him. When he finally did find him, he was with a half a dozen others his own age.

"Why you want for see me?" The belligerence was still edging his voice.

Ron met his gaze evenly. "I'd like to talk to you about our cabin."

"We no got thing for talk about. Your cabin on my land. I not have white preacher live there."

Ron waited while one of the others snickered.

"Perhaps we could rent the land from you."

"Rent land?" Guy dropped what he was doing and swaggered close to the young missionary. "Listen! You no got money enough to rent land from me! You move! Understand?"

Ron saw that there was no use in talking further with the Indian.

"If that's the way it is, we'll move the cabin just as soon as we can find a place to put it."

Guy drew himself up to his full height. "What you mean, you move cabin? You no move cabin!" He punched Ron in the chest with his forefinger. "Cabin on my land! Now it belong for me!"

The missionary stared at him incredulously. "You–you don't mean that!"

"No mean it? You try for move cabin and see! You try!"

Wearily Ron left Guy and his companions. Their raucous laughter rang in his ears as he plodded up the hill toward the little cabin that he and Darlene called home.

It was over now. Their work at High Rock was finished. No one else would let them have land on which to build a cabin after what Guy and his father had done. Not even Charlie One Bear. They would all be afraid to cross the Ferebees.

But it wouldn't make any difference if they did have land on which to build. The mission scarcely had funds to build the cabin they had. They couldn't possibly get together money enough to build another one.

Ron plodded on, mechanically putting one foot ahead of the other. The strength was gone from his legs, and his arms ached with a weariness he had never known before. But it was as nothing compared to the weariness of his mind and spirit. A deadening numbness took hold of him, and for the moment it seemed as though he didn't care anymore.

Darlene, who had been watching him from the living room window, saw the sag in his shoulders and the dejection in his walk. Hurriedly she went out to meet him.

"It can't be that bad, Ron," she said.

"Oh, couldn't it?"

Incredulously she stared at him. For an instant she thought that something had happened to make him angry with her.

"What happened?" Her lips scarcely formed the words.

Not until they were inside did he answer her.

"We have to move," he said, his voice dull and lifeless.

"That probably isn't going to be the easiest thing," she said, "but it's what we expected, isn't it?" She tried hard to sound calm and undisturbed. "We can move if they insist on it. Somebody will let us use their land, and with the boys to help, we should be able to get the cabin moved without too much trouble."

He swallowed the lump in his throat. "You don't understand," he told her. "I said that *we* have to move!"

Blankly her eyes widened.

"You mean–" She could not even bring herself to finish the sentence.

"Exactly. Guy says that the cabin is on his property, so it belongs to him. He informed me that *we* have to move and leave the cabin right where it is."

Darlene gasped. "They can't do that to us!" The fire flickered lower in her eyes as she weighed the matter. "Can they?"

No answer.

"Can they, Ron?"

Miserably, he shook his head. "I don't know what the law is about that sort of thing here in Canada," he went on. "But in the United States anything that is permanently fastened to the land becomes a part of the property and cannot be removed without the permission of the landowner."

"But that doesn't sound fair to me!"

He dropped dejectedly to a chair and slumped back, exhausted. It was almost a minute before he spoke again.

"I suppose that depends on how you look at it," he answered.

"We got permission to use the land, Ron," she said. "Doesn't that count for anything?"

"If we'd had a lease, it would count a great deal. A lease would make provision for moving the building at its expiration date providing it wasn't renewed. But we don't have anything to show that the Ferebees ever said we could build here. It would be our word against theirs."

She waited a long while before speaking, and when she did her voice was small and weak.

"What are we going to do, Ron?" she asked.

"I don't know." His voice broke. "I just don't know."

"We'll have to have a warm place to live before winter."

"And that's not too far away."

A tear escaped her eyelid and trickled, unheeded, down her cheeks. Almost mechanically they knelt to pray.

* * *

When Jim, Wade and the others came back to the cabin that night they were indignant over what had happened and were zealous for prompt, decisive action. Ernie was the first to speak his mind. "You've let 'em shove you around too long, Ron," he said. "That's one of the problems. You've got to stand up to 'em."

"That's right." Wade scooted his chair closer and leaned across the table. "How can you expect to win these characters for Christ if you don't have their respect?"

"That's what I've been tellin' Ron and Darlene!" Anger flecked Jim's voice. "You can let people walk on you about so long. Then you've got to stand up for what's right."

"It isn't going to accomplish anything if we assert our rights and lose the respect and friendship of the people in the process," Ron told them.

"Do you think people're goin' to get all shook up if you make a guy like Ferebee quit takin' advantage of you? I think you should go to the Indian agent and lay the whole thing on the line with him. I think it's time to show this Ferebee character that he's got to leave you alone."

The youthful missionary pulled in a long, deep breath and expelled the air carefully. "I had thought of doing something like that," he said.

"It's the only thing to do," Jim said.

The fellows all nodded their agreement.

"Jim's right," Ernie went on. "The Indian agent's the guy to see. He'll straighten this thing out in short order. He might even fix it so you wouldn't have to move the cabin. He might tell Ferebee to let you stay right where you are!"

Slowly Ron got to his feet. "If we could just be sure that what we decide to do is right," he said.

Darlene spoke quietly. "There's one way we can be sure," she reminded them. "We can ask God for guidance."

The discouraged little group knelt and asked God to direct Ron in his decision and to help work out the whole affair to His honor and glory. When they finished, they got stiffly to their feet. For a time, no one spoke.

At last Ron glanced at his watch. "Well, I guess we should go to bed. We've got some more work to do tomorrow."

Jim hung behind briefly after the others had gone. "I'd still show that Ferebee that he couldn't shove me around," he said.

Ron reached out and grasped Jim's shoulder. "You'd better scoot along to bed."

"OK. But I'd still stand up for my rights if I were you. I wouldn't let them do anything they wanted to without getting a little static from me."

With that he went into his bedroom leaving Ron and Darlene alone once more.

She turned to her husband. "You don't know how sorry I am about all of this, Ron."

He smiled crookedly. "It's one of those things we just have to take," he said. "God knows all about it."

"Do you have any idea what you're going to do?"

"I'm going to go and tell Ferebee that we'll move just as soon as we can."

She kissed him tenderly. "I know it's hard for you, Ron, but it's the only way."

"It may mean that we'll have to leave High Rock," he reminded her.

The lines in her face deepened. "I'd feel terrible about that," she said, "but all of these things are in God's hands. He knows the situation. If He wants us to leave here, He has something better for us somewhere else."

Ron didn't sleep much that night, and the next morning without waiting for breakfast he went to find Guy Ferebee.

"I just want to tell you that we're going to move just as soon as we find a place to move into."

The burly Indian sneered. "You no find cabin at High Rock. Nobody in village want preacher here. You move out our place you go home. No stay here anymore!"

The young missionary did not answer him.

"I give you four days for move out of my cabin. Understand? If you no move in four days we come and move you out!"

CHAPTER 8

FOREST FIRE!

The next two days passed quickly – too quickly as far as Ron and Darlene were concerned. He quit working on the cabin for the Indian evangelist and spent his time going from house to house in the settlement, talking with anyone who might have a place where they could stay.

"If we could just find something that would be suitable for us to live in for a few months," he explained to one man, "we could keep dry and warm until we could make arrangements to lease a piece of ground and build a new cabin."

Suspicion darkened the Indian man's eyes, and when he spoke his voice was cold and unfriendly. "Why you no stay in cabin you live in now?" he demanded. "Why you move?"

Ron fumbled for words. "Guy Ferebee doesn't want us to–to live there anymore," he explained weakly.

"I no want you live on my land, either. Why you no go home? Why you no preach white man's religion to white man?"

Ron would have protested that Christ died for the Indian as well as the white man, or the Black person, or the Japanese, but it was useless. Hostility flamed high in the man's black eyes.

So it went. Nobody wanted him and Darlene around. Nobody would let them stay in any building on their property, regardless of how dilapidated it was. They wanted to force him and Darlene to leave High Rock.

When he got home at night, he tried to hide his discouragement from her, but that was useless. She could read his every move.

"How did you make out?" she asked, knowing even as she did so, that it was useless.

"I didn't find a thing – not a single, solitary thing." He sat down and loosed his boots. "It's no use, Darlene. Nobody is going to let us have a place to stay. Why, I don't think we're even going to be able to find a piece of land we can build on, let alone a house to live in until we get a place."

"It will work out." She smiled hopefully.

"Sure," he said irritably. "It'll work out one way or another. It's got to. We can't stay where we are for more than two days."

She poured him some hot tea. "Perhaps the Indian evangelist and his wife can take over for a while if

we have to go," she said. "Their cabin is almost finished. They could even build the rest of it themselves
if they had to."

Ron shook his head. "I don't think the cabin would
keep them from coming, but from what I've seen of
Ralph he isn't the sort of fellow who could work suc-
cessfully alone. He told me himself that he wanted
to be with someone because he didn't know enough
about the Bible or have the necessary experience to
carry on a work alone."

"He might surprise everyone if he did take the
responsibility."

"It could be," he answered. But in his heart, he
felt the Indian would not even come to High Rock
without another missionary there to help guide and
direct his efforts.

For an hour or two Ron lay in bed that night
staring up at the ceiling. So this was the way his first
missionary venture was to end – in abject failure. He
swung his feet over the side of the bed and sat up.

This wasn't the way he and Darlene had thought
it would be like to be missionaries at all. He had been
around enough missionaries and different stations to
know that the work was hard, and he thought he was
better prepared than most to take the bitter disappointments that he knew would come their way. He had heard
missionaries tell of how hard it was to work for years
on end without seeing any visible results. He thought
he was prepared for that sort of a ministry himself, if

that was what the Lord had in store for them. But with a start he realized that he hadn't been. He hadn't known at all what it would be like to meet such opposition.

And he had had such big ideas about taking Roxie's place on the mission field, about doing the work she was supposed to have done and his own as well. Now he wouldn't be able to do anything at all. He was a failure. An absolute failure! Maybe God didn't even want him and Darlene as missionaries. Maybe that was the reason that nothing they did seemed to turn out right.

In anguish Ron dropped to his knees and began to pray.

* * *

Although there had been no clouds in the sky during the day, there was a thunderstorm during the night. It didn't rain much, but there was a great deal of lightning. And when they got up the next morning a thin sliver of smoke was twisting upward in the still air from a spot across the big lake.

Jim saw it first. He watched it for a moment or two, curiously. "Ron," he called, "come here for a minute, will you?"

Ron came up and stood beside him. "What is it, Jim?"

The boy moved a few paces to one side, still staring intently across the lake. "Is that smoke coming from somebody's cabin?"

Ron shook his head. "It couldn't be. Nobody lives over there."

"Do you suppose some fishermen got careless and let a fire get away?"

"There aren't any sport fishermen around here," Ron said. "That must have been started by lightning."

Darlene heard him and came to the door. "What is it, Ron?"

"Forest fire."

"That isn't good, is it?'"

"As dry as it's been, it could be plenty bad."

"Do you suppose anyone has seen it?" Jim asked.

"I'm sure they have, but we'll have to go down to the Bay store, just in case. There's a transmitter there so they can get word out."

When they reached the store, however, a dozen or so men had gathered and were tensely watching the smoke. The Hudson Bay manager came out to them.

"I just got through to Prince Albert," he said. "The Department of Natural Resources will have a man up here in a couple of hours."

One of the Indians swore darkly. "Field officer come, first thing he do, he close lake for fishing. Just now when it get good."

The Hudson Bay manager eyed him critically. "What're you kickin' about? You'll get paid for fightin' the fire."

The dark-skinned Cree swore again. "We get pay for fight fire, but who want for fight fire when fishing is good?"

They went back into the store and a few minutes later the radio was crackling again. Joe went back to talk on it. "This is Zero Five Eight Three," he answered. "Over."

"Hello, Joe. This is Bert."

"How are you?"

"How do you expect a fellow to be with fires all over? Got any men up there?"

"The usual bunch."

"You'd better appoint a foreman and have a crew get over on that fire. I'll be there as soon as I can. Probably before the day is out. Over."

"I'll take care of it right away. Want any men to stand by? Over."

"I'll have to have at least a dozen," the field officer said crisply. "And put up some grub for them before I get there so we can get on the fire without losing any time. Over and out."

Ron, who had been standing near the transmitter, turned to the Hudson Bay manager. "Is there anything we can do?" he asked.

"You'll have to see about that when Bert gets here. He'll be in charge, you know."

Joe got several men to go across the lake immediately and start fighting the fire. Bert Davis flew into the settlement shortly before noon, surveyed the fire and dispatched the rest of the men who had gathered at the store.

"That blaze is getting a better start than I thought

it would, Joe," he said. "If it gets up in that jack pine on the ridge, we'll be in for plenty of trouble."

The Indian chief, who had joined them moments before, nodded gravely. "How many men you want?"

"Everybody."

There was a brief hesitation. "Not much men in settlement. Men fishing."

"Have them come in."

"They no like leaving nets for fight fire."

The government official's eyes snapped. "They won't be fishing after today. I'm closing the lake to fishing until the fire's out."

Guy pushed up to him belligerently. "You no do that. You got no right for close the lake."

"I've already closed it. Now get your gear and get down to the dock! You're going over there in half an hour."

"I have nets out."

"You've had a boy helping you. He can lift them and bring them in."

The big fellow glared angrily at the DNR official but did as he was told.

Presently Ron went up to the field officer and introduced himself. "There are five of us. We'll be glad to help if you need us."

"Thanks." The officer's face softened slightly. "Right now, I think we've got about all the help we'll need unless the flames get out of hand. Since I had to close the lake to fishing, I'm obligated to use all the fishermen to fight the fire. But if we should need you, we'll call on you."

Ron and the others went back to the cabin they had been building and set to work, but they could not keep their eyes or their minds off the fire across the lake. The smoke was billowing upward in ever-increasing clouds, and by midafternoon the wind began to build.

Wade laid his hammer on the step and moved to a vantage point where he had an unrestricted view of the fire. "That fire's movin' awful fast, Ron," he said. "It's four times as big as it was this morning."

Even as they watched, flames thrashed above the trees.

"Boy, you can say that again. It must have gotten up into the jack pine Bert was talking about."

"Think they'll have to get us to help fight the fire?"

The young missionary shrugged his shoulders. "If they need us," he said, "I'll be glad to go. But I don't mind telling you that I don't look forward to going out on the fire line. I've done some of it. It's not what it's cracked up to be."

When they finished work on the cabin that evening, they stopped by the Hudson Bay store on the way back to the Orlis home. Mr. Davis had taken over the radio transmitter and was directing the firefighting from there. Ron approached the trading post manager.

"How's it going?" he asked.

"Not too good. Bert called Prince Albert for a water bomber and a helicopter, but they've got so many fires they couldn't send anything to us right now. That means he's got to fight it from the ground."

"It's in the jack pine, isn't it?"

The Hudson Bay man nodded. "It sure is. And it's really giving them firefighters plenty of trouble. Bert can't keep in touch with them by radio more than half the time."

"A fire moving like that one is hard enough to keep away from, let alone do much fighting."

Joe went over and poured himself a cup of coffee, liberally lacing it with canned milk. "I'm just mighty glad that I'm not out there," he said. "It's going to be a long, hard night."

A few minutes later the DNR officer looked up. Concern marred the blue of his eyes. "I can't get in touch with Guy Ferebee and his crew," he said. "I haven't heard from them for a couple of hours."

Ron noted the fear in his voice. "Do you think their radio could be out of whack?" he asked.

"Could be. But things were getting mighty hot for them when I last talked to them. I don't like this, Orlis. That fire could have them trapped!"

CHAPTER 9

CHRISTIANS VOLUNTEER

Mr. Davis bent over the radio transmitter once more. "This is H D Zero Four calling Six One," he said crisply. "Come in, Six One. Over."

The only sound was the crackling of static.

"This is H D Zero Four calling Six One. Come in, Six One. Come in, Six One. Over."

As he looked up, Ron spoke to him. "Still can't get them?"

The field officer shook his head. "I've been trying for the last fifteen minutes, but they don't answer."

Once more he directed his attention to the radio phone. "This is H D Zero Four calling anyone on jack pine fire. This is H D Zero Four calling anyone on jack pine fire. Come in, anyone on jack pine fire. Over."

A faint voice broke through the static. "This is Seven Five calling H D Zero Four. What's the trouble, Bert? Over."

"I've been trying to make contact with Guy Ferebee. Haven't heard from him for over three hours. Have you seen or heard anything of him or his boys? Over."

"Not a thing since he went into the bush the same time we did. Of course, we haven't had much time to look for anyone."

"What's it like over there? Over."

"I'm telling you, Bert, this is as bad a fire as I've seen for fifteen years. We've had about all we could do just stayin' out of its way. What about that water bomber? When are they going to get here to give us some help? Over."

"Prince Albert says we'll have one first thing in the morning," Bert went on, "providing they can get one of the other fires under control enough to spare it."

"That's not goin' to do us much good," the firefighter said cryptically. "By that time, she'll have half the country between here and Cree Lake afire. Better tell 'em to get a move on if they don't want to burn up this end of Saskatchewan. Over."

"Where are you now, Ed? Over."

"We're halfway between the ridge and Lake Salligan." He paused so long that Davis thought he had lost contact and broke in to call him again. "Sorry, Bert. I've just been doin' some thinkin'. If that wind and this dandy little fire of yours will cooperate, we'll stay where we are. If they don't, we're goin' to be running, and that's for sure. Over."

"Try to contact Ferebee from over there, will you?

If his batteries are weak, you might be able to read him where we couldn't. Over."

"Roger, Bert. We'll do the best we can to get hold of him. But if you hear us squeal for help, we'll be in bad trouble and'll be needin' you, pronto. Over and out."

The DNR officer turned off the radio transmitter but continued to monitor Ed as the firefighter tried to contact Guy Ferebee from the other side of the lake.

"This is Seven Five calling Six One. This is Seven Five calling Six One. Come in, Ferebee. Come in, Ferebee. Over."

There was no response.

A moment or two later he repeated the call. Still there was no answer. The DNR officer frowned, the lines deep on his ashen face.

"It's no use," he said miserably. "Ed can't get in touch with them either."

"You know Ferebee," Joe put in. "He might not even have his radio turned on."

"Could be. But we can't count on that. There might be another reason for our not being able to get in touch with him and his men."

"It doesn't sound good," Ron said, "does it?"

"That's for sure." He sighed deeply.

The Hudson Bay manager was called to the front of the store. It was a moment or two before he came back to where Ron and Bert were standing.

"That chopper would sure come in handy right now, wouldn't it," he said.

"You can say that again. But we're not going to get either the chopper or the water bomber until morning at the very earliest, and like Ed said, by that time it may be too late."

There was a long, painful silence.

"It doesn't sound as though the men are able to do much over there, does it?" Joe asked.

"You can't make any progress fighting a fire like that with the number of men we've got and no equipment to help them." He sat down at the radio again and fingered the key uneasily. "I wish we had pulled the men out of there. We'd let it go until we can get some equipment to help us."

The Hudson Bay manager eyed him critically. "If you were going to pull them out, how'd you go about it?"

"We could get Ed by radio, but I don't know how we'd ever get in touch with Guy Ferebee. He's too far from Ed for him to get hold of him, and the fire's in between them." He breathed deeply. "The trouble is there's no one left to go over after them unless I go myself. Everyone else is committed over there."

"You can't leave," Joe said. "You're needed here." Mr. Davis glanced at him disapprovingly but said nothing. That was the way it was on fires. Everyone in the area was a self-styled expert who felt the DNR officer didn't know his job – and especially if he happened to be as young as he was.

Ron spoke up quickly. "If you need someone to go over and get those fellows, we can go."

The other two men stared at him.

"What do you know about forest fires?" the field officer demanded.

"I was raised in northern Minnesota. I've been on the fire line plenty of times."

The officer tugged thoughtfully at the lobe of his ear. "What about the boys who've been helping you?" he asked. "What do they know about the woods?"

"The older fellows haven't had any experience to speak of," Ron went on, "but Jim Morgan has had some. He lived with my parents and my older brother for several years. He knows how to take care of himself in the woods."

Bert glanced out the window at the still-lit sky. "We've still got a couple of hours of daylight left," he said. "Joe, do you think you can get some boats and motors for us?"

"Sure thing." The Hudson Bay manager grabbed his Siwash sweater and pulled it on as he started for the door. "I'll be back in a few minutes."

Ron called after him. "Stop by my cabin and have Darlene get the fellows over here right away."

Mr. Davis was already on the radio telling Ed to bring his men out to the lake.

"Boats will be there to pick you up in an hour, Ed. Over."

"That's the best news we've heard since you sent us over here and dumped us, Bert Boy. We'll be waiting. Don't disappoint us. Over."

Ron was already studying the map.

"You won't have any trouble finding Ed," Mr. Davis told him. "He's a good woodsman. He'll have his men out to the lake when you get there."

"But what about Ferebee? Where will he be?"

"I don't have any idea at the moment." The officer studied the map. "We let them off here." He pointed to a small cove not far from the place where the fire started. "But the way that fire's gone, it's hard to say which way they've been forced to go." He paused momentarily. "Guy's a good woodsman and an excellent firefighter. Probably as good as we have at High Rock. I think he'd have kept his men in this area near the lake – or perhaps over here. Either place would be easier to keep the men together."

"Those places are out of the jack pine, aren't they?

Davis nodded. "They're both out of the jack pine. We can be thankful for that. The fire won't be quite so bad in those areas."

Ron nodded. "It sounds reasonable that they'd be in one place or the other," he said, "if they didn't get cut off before they got across the ridge." He studied the map again. "Now, just exactly what is it that you want us to do, Bert?"

"Take the boats and go over to this point, Ron," he directed. "Search along the northwest shore. They may be in one of these little bays. I'll get on the radio and tell Ed to bring his gang out to meet you. I'll tell him you'll pick them up before dark."

Ron and the DNR officer got some food and took it down to the dock.

"I've got to contact Prince Albert again at eight o'clock," he said. "As soon as I give them my report, I'll bring Joe and come over to help."

"Good deal."

By the time they got down to the dock, the Hudson Bay manager, Jim, and the CBI students had arrived with the boats.

"They're all gassed and ready to go."

Ron nodded, but he was looking out across the wide expanse of water. The wind was beginning to howl through the trees and scuff the placid lake surface. It wouldn't be long until the white caps would be showing. It would be a rough, dangerous crossing.

Jim jumped lightly out of the boat.

"All set, Ron," he said crisply. "How do you want us to pair off?"

"You can take Ray with you," the missionary said. "Wade and Ernie can go together. I'll go alone."

Before they got into their boats, they bowed their heads for prayer. Mr. Davis and the Hudson Bay man watched them curiously but were quiet until they finished.

"Dear God," Ron prayed aloud, "thank You for the way You have watched over us in the past; for the way You have guided us and directed us. Now, we come to You again, asking that You will keep each of us safe during this trip. We're especially concerned about the fellows on the fire line. We pray that You will keep them safe and guide us to them now. In Your name and for Your sake we ask it. Amen."

With that Ron checked to see that they all had life jackets. Only then did he get into his boat. The field officer waved to them.

"Take care of yourselves. I'll be over there in a couple of hours."

Ron started the engine and headed toward the spot that Mr. Davis had marked on the map. The smoke was getting thicker and pressed close to the water, even as the wind continued to build. It was going to be a rough, wet crossing. Ron's eyes narrowed as a huge breaker quartered over the prow, spilling half a tub full of water inside.

Quickly he reached for the bailing bucket. A couple more like that and the water would be ankle-deep in the bottom of the heavy, flat-bottom scow. He was glad he had Jim in one of the other boats. Jim would know how important it was to get the water out. He could only pray that Wade and Ernie would do the same.

Ron paused in his bailing long enough to glance at the other boats. Both Wade and Jim's companion, Ray, were bailing furiously.

Then Ron set to work again. With an eye on the waves, he held the boat angled into them as he continued to bail until he had most of the water out.

By this time, the smoke was so thick he could

scarcely make out the opposite shore. The sun shone through the smoky overcast, a huge copper ball that cast an eerie sheen across the water.

His eyes burned and he began to cough. He had forgotten the acrid smell of the smoke, the ash that settled over everything, the way his nose and throat pinched until he could scarcely breathe. It had been years since he had been in a forest fire, but everything came back with a rush. It seemed like only yesterday that he and Danny had been helping fight fire.

The closer they got to shore the lower the waves were, but that meant the force of the wind had lessened and the smoke was noticeably worse.

Ron looked at his companions in the boats on either side. Already the soot and ash that was drifting down like black snow was clinging to their sweating faces and smudging their clothes.

He slowed his motor and motioned to Ernie and Jim to do the same. They were in a hurry, which was true, but hurry or not, a careful woodsman didn't go slamming around near a strange shore where there might be rocks to ruin his outboard motor or his boat.

When they were close enough so the water was calm, Ron shut off the outboard and reached for the map. The map wouldn't do much good in smoke so thick that the contour of the shoreline could not be seen, but still he studied it carefully.

For the first time his heart faltered, and his mouth went dry and cottony. How were they going to be able to find Ferebee and his men if they weren't able to make their way down to the lakeshore?

"Ron!" Jim's voice sounded hollow and far away. "Ron! Where are you?"

"Right here!" he shouted.

In a moment Jim's boat crept into view and the boy shut off the slow-running motor.

"That scared us for a minute!" he exclaimed. "We didn't know where you were."

For a time, Ron did not speak.

"What're we going to do, Ron?" Jim asked. "How're we goin' to find those guys in this stuff?"

CHAPTER 10

SEARCH FOR FIREFIGHTERS

For a minute or two Ron and his companions sat motionless in their boats, staring blankly into the thick, acrid smoke. Ron felt the muscles in his throat constrict, as though they were being squeezed by an invisible hand. He coughed and rubbed at his smarting eyes. This was something he hadn't counted on.

A desperate, wordless prayer for help and wisdom escaped his heart. The fellows were all looking at him wonderingly for direction, but what could he tell them?

At last Jim repeated his question. "What're we going to do?" he asked, concern edging his voice. "How're we going to find them in this?"

Ron was slow in answering. "They'll have to come out to the lakeshore." He hoped he sounded more convincing than he felt. "All we have to do is to cruise along the shore until we find them. It might not be such a difficult job at all."

Ernie glanced up at the darkening sky.

"We shouldn't have too much trouble finding them if they can make it before dark."

Wade swallowed hard.

"We–we aren't going to have to separate, are we?" he asked, his voice breaking.

The young missionary hesitated. That was exactly what he had planned to do when they left High Rock. He had figured they would cross the big lake together, and once on the side nearest the fires he had planned on having them go in different directions in order to cover the largest amount of territory in the shortest possible time.

But he had not reckoned on the smoke lying like a London fog over the area until it blotted out the shore and every landmark.

Wade spoke again, fearfully. "If we get into trouble in this stuff we'll be dead ducks. Nobody'll be able to find us," he said.

"I think it's best to stick together," Ron assured him. "I'll take the lead. You fellows can follow me."

He started his outboard motor once more and inched slowly forward until he was close enough to make out the blurred, shadowy shapes of the trees on shore. Then he turned and moved parallel to them. Every now and then he stopped and called out, loudly.

"Hello-o-o-o! Hello-o-o-o-o!" His voice echoed and reechoed through the murky curtain of smoke. "Guy!" he shouted. "Guy Ferebee! Are you there?"

But there was no answer. All was silent except for the crackling of the fire in the distance and the mournful moaning of the wind in the trees.

Although it was so dark that they could not see it falling, the ash was drifting down to cling to their faces and clothing and to freckle the water around the boats. Ron wiped his hand across his face and looked at it, grimy and smeared with soot.

He called out loudly once more to the firefighters, but the wind seized his voice and flung it back at him.

Time moved slowly, and with each passing minute the darkness grew a shade deeper. The red glow in the sky was the sun that moved farther and farther down behind the rim of trees, and the smoke seemed thicker than ever.

Although Ron scarcely realized it, he had to keep moving closer to shore so they could keep the trees that lined the beach in sight.

They poked along the smoke-shrouded shore for a mile or more, calling out to the firefighters and straining their eyes to catch some sign of movement along the beach. But darkness closed in relentlessly and they had seen nothing of the young Indian firefighters.

At last Ron stopped and motioned the other two boats to come up alongside.

"What do you think?" he asked.

Jim spoke up quickly. "I don't think we've got a chance of finding them in this stuff, Ron. We couldn't see them if we came within a hundred yards of them."

Wade agreed.

"I think you're right, Jim. We couldn't see them in this stuff unless we stumbled over them."

Before Ron could answer, the crackling of the fire in the trees became a roar and the flames leaped high against the darkening sky. The entire area was bathed in an eerie orange glow.

Fear stabbed deeply into the young missionary's heart. How could men live in an inferno like that? What had happened to Guy Ferebee and the fellows who had gone up to the fire line with him?

"We'll just have to keep looking," Ron said. "They may be along here anywhere."

They continued to look for the lost firefighters until darkness closed in on them.

Jim tried to make out the shore but could not. "What do you think now, Ron?" he asked. "What are we going to do?"

Reluctantly Ron spoke. "There's no use in our staying here now and trying to find them. We can't see a thing. All we'll do is wreck a propeller or smash a hole in one of our boats on a rock."

"But we can't just stop looking for them, Ron!" Jim's voice rose to a crescendo. "It's like Bert said, every minute counts. We've got to keep looking for them until we find them."

"We can't do it!" There was finality in Ron's voice. "In the first place, it's so dark now we could pass right by them and not even know they were there."

"We could go ashore and–and look for them," Jim suggested. "I'd rather try that than quit hunting for them altogether."

"And get into a bad spot ourselves?" Ron asked. "That wouldn't help Guy Ferebee or anyone else. We're going back out to one of the islands we passed on the way in and spend the night. As soon as it's daylight we'll have a chance of seeing something. Then we'll come back and look again."

"That makes sense to me," Ray put in.

The others voiced their agreement.

"I suppose it does," Jim acknowledged, "but I know how I'd feel if I were trapped in a forest fire and the guys who were looking for me would just quit for awhile."

"It's the best thing, Jim," Ron said, starting his outboard motor once more. "Believe me." He headed slowly away from the mainland toward one of the islands. "Follow me, fellas," he said, "and whatever you do, stay close. We could get separated from each other very easily in this muck. Then we'd have someone else to hunt for."

He led them out to a small island a mile or so from shore and they pulled their boats up on the sandy beach and proceeded to make camp for the night.

Ernie and Ray got the blankets out of the prow while Wade and Jim got the food. Ron was already building a small fire.

They ate, but not because they were hungry. The smoke and darkness and the concern for the firefighters on the mainland had stolen whatever appetite they might have had.

Jim could talk of but little else.

"I sure wish we knew where those guys were and if they're all right," he said. "I'd feel a lot better about leaving them out there."

"They're experienced in the woods," Ray said. "And they've all lived up here all their lives, so they know about fighting fires. They should be able to stay out of the way of it."

"If the fire didn't manage to get around behind them," Jim continued. "I've only been around a couple of forest fires, but I tell you, they're rough. You don't know what they're going to do."

Ron took his New Testament from his pocket.

"We'd better get some sleep. We're all going to need it. But before we do, let's have a little time of Bible reading and prayer."

He read to them from the fourteenth chapter of the book of John and afterward they had a period of prayer. Each one in the tense little group took his turn praying, asking for God's help for the men fighting the fire.

Presently they stretched out near their own little campfire, pulling their blankets around them, and tried to sleep. All, that was, except Ron. He stood motionless for an hour or more, staring into the flames. The only time he moved was to stir the coals or put in more wood. Sometime after midnight he went down to the boats and sat on the nose of the one he had been using.

He was still sitting there when Jim woke up toward morning and went looking for him.

"Oh, there you are, Ron."

The young missionary bolted. "Jim!" he exclaimed. "What're you doing up at this time of night?"

"I came looking for you."

"I'm all right," Ron told him. "You'd better go back to bed. We've got a big day ahead of us."

"That's just what I was thinking. You'd better get some sleep, too."

A sigh escaped his lips. "To tell you the truth I don't feel much like sleeping. I keep wondering if I did the right thing in calling off the search and bringing you fellows over here last night."

"You remember what Dad Orlis used to tell us when we got to talking that way, don't you?"

Ron eyed him curiously. "I'm not sure."

"He always said that the best way to handle any problem is to pray about it, do what you feel is best according to the way God is leading, and then not to worry about it."

A faint smile toyed with the corner of Ron's mouth. "Thanks, Jim," he said, "that's just what I needed." With that he turned and went back to the fire, wrapping himself in a blanket. In a few minutes he was fast asleep.

As soon as it was light, however, he got the fellows up and out to the boats again. "We'll go over to this little bay." He indicated a spot on the map. "Then we'll go down the river for a mile or so. There's a chance they could have gone across the swamp in this direction."

They went over to the mainland and skirted the shore in the direction of the bay. Now that it was daylight and there was only smoke shrouding the area, they could see much better. They had only been traveling a few minutes when Jim let out a shout. "Ron!" he cried. "Look over there!"

Ron stared as though he could scarcely believe what he was seeing. A dozen men or so were huddled together on the lakeshore. The fire was on the narrow ridge not more than fifty or sixty yards behind them!

CHAPTER 11

GOD'S WAYS ARE DIFFERENT

The men on shore started to wave and shout. Two or three waded knee-deep into the water.

Jim turned gleefully to Ron. "We've found them! We've found them!"

For an answer Ron breathed a prayer. "Thank You, Lord! Thank You!"

The bedraggled firefighters were laughing and shouting excitedly as the boats turned in toward shore. Only Guy Ferebee remained aloof. He stood to one side, glaring darkly at Ron and his companions. But Ron didn't seem to notice. He was too busy watching the bottom for rocks.

"Keep your eyes open, fellas," he warned. "We don't want to take a chance on ruining a prop now."

Cautiously he guided his boat into shore. Jim and Wade followed close behind him. Eager hands reached out to grasp the prow of the boat.

"Are we glad to see you!" one of the young Indians exclaimed. "We didn't know whether anyone was goin' to come over after us or not!"

The speaker scrambled into the boat. In a moment or two everyone was climbing into one boat or another. Even Guy came over and hoisted himself into Ron's craft.

The young missionary looked anxiously about. "Is everybody here, Guy?" he asked.

Guy spoke up, scorn coloring his voice. "Everybody here," he snorted. "Sure everybody here. You no think I take men into woods and come back without them, do you?"

Ron did not answer. He looked over at the other two boats.

"Everybody in?" The answer to his question choked off as the high-pitched whine of a large outboard motor drifted in.

"Somebody else's coming!" Jim shouted.

Guy straightened, listening intently.

"DNR boat!" he announced.

Half a minute later Mr. Davis roared into sight and headed for them. As he sped close to shore, he cut off the motor.

"I see you found them, Ron!" the field officer exclaimed.

"We just got here."

"Good enough. Anybody want to ride with me?"

The tall Indian who had been in charge of the fire-fighters jumped out of Ron's boat into knee-deep water. Hatred still gleamed in his eyes. "I'll go with him!"

Mr. Davis took several others to equalize the loads, and the four boats roared back across the lake in the direction of High Rock.

"What about Ed and his men?" Jim asked the DNR officer when they reached the settlement on the other side of the lake.

"We found them last night," he said. "They're all here in High Rock now."

* * *

The next afternoon Ron and Darlene stood at the dock watching the mission plane take off with Jim and Ray. The other two had gone out on the plane that morning. It was several minutes before Darlene was able to speak.

"I sort of hate to see them leave," she said.

Ron put his arm tenderly around her shoulders. "So do I." He paused. "It's going to be mighty lonely around here without them – especially without Jim. I'm going to miss that little shrimp."

Almost mechanically they turned and started up the path to their little cabin.

"I'm so glad you were able to find those men, Ron," Darlene said.

"So am I."

"I prayed and prayed that you would find them so that we'd be able to demonstrate to the people here in the village that we're their friends and want to help them," she went on. "Do you suppose it'll have any effect on Guy's decision to make us move?"

Ron shook his head. "You can never tell about someone like Guy, of course," he said. "He might be swayed by something like this, but I have my doubts. He didn't seem to be very glad to see that we were the ones who had found him and his men."

They hadn't been back at their cabin for more than a few minutes when there was a knock at the door.

"I'll answer it," Darlene said.

"It's probably for me."

Wearily Ron went to open it. Guy Ferebee was standing there staring at him.

"*Waaci*," Ron said.

"*Waaci*," the big Indian replied without warmth in his voice.

"Won't you come in?" In spite of the other's apparent unfriendliness Ron managed a smile as he opened the screen door.

"I come for see you."

"Fine. Come on in and have some tea with us. Darlene just about has it ready."

Still the Indian did not move.

"When you plan for leave?" Guy demanded.

"That's something I'd like to talk to you about. We haven't been able to find another place to live."

"I need cabin."

"I'm sure I can locate something if we only have a couple of more days to look around."

There was a brief pause. Guy's jaw was granite hard. "You have too much time already. You not find place for live in High Rock. Nobody want you here! You leave tomorrow!"

"We can't possibly leave tomorrow," Ron said, striving to keep the desperation from his voice. "If we can't get a place to stay here, we'll have to pack our things and make arrangements for the mission plane to come up after us. That'll take more than a day or two."

Guy drew himself up to his full height and expelled his breath slowly. "In two days you be gone! Hear me?" With that he turned on his heel and stormed off the porch.

Darlene came up beside her husband. She was as concerned as he was. "Ron," she said softly, "what are we going to do?"

He put his arm around her shoulder and pulled her close to him, seeming to draw strength from her very nearness. "What can we do?" he asked with desperate weariness. "We've got to leave!"

They went back into the house presently and sat down in the living room for a long while, talking in low tones. At last Ron got to his feet.

"We've been praying for an answer, Darlene," he said. "This seems to be it."

She nodded, but there were tears lingering just behind her eyelashes.

"But to have to leave when we know that the people at High Rock need the gospel so badly," she said. "It doesn't seem right, somehow."

"God knows all about it, Darlene. We've asked Him for the answer to our problem here. Now He's given it. The least we can do is to accept it."

"But perhaps Satan is the one who is trying to get us so discouraged that we will leave here," she said. "Or perhaps God is allowing us to be tested. You don't think there's anyone else in High Rock who'll let us move into a cabin or any kind of a shack until we can get another place of our own?"

He shook his head. "I've talked to every person in the settlement. I've even pleaded with some of them to let us have a place." He sounded as though he had no will to continue struggling. "You can't imagine the hostility there is against the gospel, Darlene. The people all seem to want us to leave."

She pursed her lips. "Do–do you think the folks at headquarters will understand?" she asked. "Will they know that we've done the very best we could?"

Ron nodded. "Sure they will. They know these people better than we do, and Mr. Dunbar has been flying in and out of here all the time. He knows what we're up against."

"But so much time and effort and money has gone into the work here. It seems a shame to turn our back on it and let it all be wasted."

"I don't imagine this is the first time the mission has tried to open up a station that hasn't gone. The people there know how hard it is to break through the prejudice and distrust that's been built up over the years." He went across the room and sat down again. "Now the average Christian back home is something else again. Too many of them have the idea that the people in places like this are sitting here waiting for someone to come and bring the gospel to them. And once they hear it, they will flock to services, confess their sin and plead to be baptized; when that isn't the way it is at all."

"When are you going to radio for the plane?"

He glanced at his watch. "It's too late to do it now. We'll have to take care of that first thing in the morning. I only hope Mr. Dunbar is able to come up right away."

They went to bed at the usual time that night, but neither of them slept. As soon as the Hudson Bay store opened the next morning Ron went down and radioed for the plane to come up after them. The store manager came over to the radio as soon as Ron had finished and leaned against the shelves.

"So, you're goin' to be leavin' us," he said curiously. Ron nodded.

"Goin' out on holiday?"

"No, I guess we'll be leaving for good."

Joe's lips pursed. "I thought you come up here to stay. I didn't figure you'd be gettin' sick of the country so soon."

"That's not it at all. We haven't been able to find a place where we can live, and Guy Ferebee says we can't stay where we are. So, we don't have any choice. We've got to leave."

The Hudson Bay manager took a deep breath.

"Why don't you see the Indian agent about it? These lyin' Indians won't face up to him with their stories. If Ferebee gave you his word that you could build on his land, the agent'll get to the bottom of it and let you stay where you are."

"We've thought about that," Ron replied, "but we've decided that we don't want to stay on that basis."

The store manager shook his head. "Why not? Answer me that?"

"Well, we want to be a Christian example to the people. We can't lead them to Christ if we insist on our rights all the way through."

"I never have gone much for religion," Joe went on, "but I'm going to hate to see you two leave. Your lives really seem to mean something."

Ron went back to the little cabin after getting some boxes for their things and making arrangements for the Hudson Bay manager to keep them until the winter freeze-up when the "cat trains" begin to come in.

Darlene was busy packing when he reached the cabin.

"How are things going?" he asked.

"All right, I guess." She looked up, misery written on her young face. "Somehow, this doesn't seem to be happening. I–I can hardly believe that it's true."

"It's true, all right." He sat down heavily. "Charlie One Bear was in the store this morning when I sent the message. He went out without even speaking to me."

She shook her head. "I still can't understand how these people can be so-so hard that they would force us to leave High Rock the way they are. All we've ever done since we came here has been to try to help them."

"But they don't realize that," he said, getting to his feet. "I suppose we'd better keep at it. The plane'll be here right after dinner. And we've got to have all of this stuff packed and over to the Hudson Bay store before we leave."

The minutes seemed to drag by as they worked. At last they finished packing the last box and Ron was starting for the door when there was a firm knock outside. Darlene looked at him.

"You don't suppose the plane's here already, do you?" she asked.

"I don't see how it could be. He wasn't supposed to leave there until about one-thirty or two o'clock."

The young missionary set the box down and opened the door. There stood the village chief and Charlie One Bear. Behind them were Guy Ferebee and his father. Briefly Ron forgot his manners and stared at them.

"We want for talk with you," the chief said, his voice cold and expressionless.

Ron stepped aside so they could come in.

"We're all torn up here and have everything packed or we'd offer you some tea."

The chief only grunted. It was a moment or two before he spoke. This time there was a different tone in his voice – one Ron had never heard before.

"Charlie One Bear come for see me this morning," he said. "He tell me what happen at his cabin one night. How you came and make the young men leave him and his family alone." He paused significantly. "I not know until today that Guy say you move."

"The plane will be here for us in a couple of hours," Ron said.

"You are friend of our people," the chief said. "You come for help us."

"That's what we wanted to do," Ron told him, "but we have to leave. We have no place to stay."

"Ferebee give his word you could build cabin on his land. It not good when man break his word." With that he turned deliberately to Guy Ferebee. "You tell him what you came for to say."

The young Indian glared at the chief and then at Ron. When he did not speak, the chief continued.

"This white man and his friends help when you trapped by fire. They good friends of our people."

Young Ferebee snarled. "The DNR plane was there five minutes later. We would have gotten out, all right."

"But you not know the DNR was close. Neither did he." The chief pointed to Ron with a nod of his head. "He and his friends go out to hunt for you after you do wrong to him. Now tell him, or I tell him for you."

The older Ferebee broke in. "What chief say is true. We have decide you stay."

Guy Ferebee was as belligerent as ever, yet under the penetrating stare of the chief he spoke.

"I make mistake when I say you should leave. My father give you his word. You make out paper. We sign so you can stay."

Ron and Darlene stared at him as though they could scarcely believe what he was saying.

"You mean you've changed your mind and we can go on living here?"

"We sign paper."

The chief spoke up suddenly.

"No need for paper. You give word before One Bear. You give word before me. There be no trouble. White man and his wife, they stay." With that they turned and left as quickly as they had come.

Ron stared after them. For a moment it was all he could do to keep his eyes from filling with tears.

"Did you hear them, Darlene?" He spoke in hushed tones, as though the very sound of his voice might break the spell. "They said we can stay!"

She tried to speak but could not. Instead, she dropped to a chair and for a moment or two, sobbed out her relief.

Ron went over and put his arm comfortingly around her shoulder.

"Isn't it wonderful?" he exclaimed. "We can stay here at High Rock. God wants us to serve Him here after all."

It was some time before Darlene could say a word. And when she did her voice was taut and quavering.

"Oh, Ron," she said, "while you and the boys were out on the lake trying to find the firefighters,

I prayed and prayed that the Lord would use it to open the hearts of these people to the gospel. But I thought He would touch Guy Ferebee or one of the other firefighters. I didn't once expect the chief to come into it."

"God doesn't always answer our prayers in exactly the way we expect Him to."

There was a brief silence.

"Only," she went on, "it still seems that nobody is interested in the gospel."

"Honey, we're here in one of the strongholds of Satan. We can't expect them to come through the first time they hear the gospel. Why, back home people don't come to Christ that easily. And they've heard the gospel repeatedly. They haven't hardened their hearts nearly as much as the trappers and fishermen up here at High Rock."

She smiled at him through her tears. "At least they know that we're their friends now," she said. "There's that much in our favor."

"That's right. And we've made a big step forward when the chief comes out for us. That means that none of these men are going to dare to stand up against us and try to give us any real trouble again. Our position here is finally secure."

"God has His purpose in allowing us to stay here, Ron," she said. "That means we *are* going to be able to win some of them for Him sooner or later."

He nodded and looked back over at the boxes.

"You know," he told her, "it's sure going to be a lot easier to unpack this stuff than it was to pack it."

He stood suddenly and reached for his jacket. "I just thought of something. I've got to get down and radio headquarters so they can stop the mission plane. There's no need for Mr. Dunbar to make a trip up here for nothing."

THE
DANNY ORLIS SERIES

The Danny Orlis series, by Bernard Palmer, delivers a blend of adventure, mystery, and suspense through various settings—from the Canadian wilderness to Guatemalan jungles. Danny Orlis, an adept outdoorsman, skilled athlete, and committed Christian, employs his quick thinking, calm bravery, and biblical solutions to confront everyday problems and hair-raising dangers. Early stories focus on Danny navigating school life, sports, and outdoor challenges, while in later books, Danny and his wife Kay provide wisdom and guidance to youngsters facing lifelike situations and challenges. Having sold over two million copies, this series has made Palmer a renowned author in Christian youth literature. Palmer is also the author of the Felicia Cartright series and various other series for Christian youth.

AVAILABLE FROM WWW.ANEKOPRESS.COM

www.ingramcontent.com/pod-product-compliance
Lightning Source LLC
Chambersburg PA
CBHW060504300726
48975CB00008B/2636